HOUSE OF MIRACLES

STRONG INDEPENDENT WOMEN SERIES
BOOK 1

TIERNEY JAMES

Publishing Coordinator – Sharon Kizziah-Holmes

Paperback-Press
an imprint of
Paperback Press, LLC

ISBN -13: 978-1-964559-10-0

DEDICATION

This book is dedicated to all those who serve children that have nothing. They are the true angels that walk among us as they spread hope and goodwill.

ACKNOWLEDGMENTS

Paperback Press – Thank you for yet another great experience and your tireless work you give not only to me, but all your authors. You make my job stress free each time we work together.

Decadent Publishing Editors – Kate Richards and Nan Sipe always make me a better writer. It is always a joy to work with these editors and see their vision. I also appreciate their encouragement and belief in my work.

Sweet & Spicey Designs – Jaycee DeLorenzo always is ready to listen to my ideas and create the next great cover art. She now has managed to do all my covers and I'm 100% thrilled at her work.

Lipstick & Danger Street Team – Thank you for always getting the word out about my books, reading the ARCs and participating in my reader group.

CHAPTER 1

"Don't look down," he yelled. "Grab my hand. I'll pull you up!"

Meredith sobbed as she disobeyed and stole a glance down the face of the cliff to the waves crashing against the rocks below. "I can't." She clung to the two protruding rocks the size of a softball, a foot apart. They were sharp and wet. Clinging to them, her body smashed against the rugged face of the cliff. The rain and wind intensified just as a crash of lightning forced a scream to escape from deep inside her.

"Meredith, it's now or never. Trust me."

He reached down farther than he should have, his body extended over the edge. If she reached up, she would have to release her grip on the protruding rock. This would unsteady her body.

"Meredith!"

As she opened her mouth, a blast of rain slammed into her face like tiny razor blades. All she could do was nod and wiggle her fingers in hopes of tightening her grip. In slow motion, she eased one hand free, only

1

to slip and grab her safety rock once more. With her head resting against the rocky surface, she could hear his encouragement, edged with desperation.

"Remember. Take a deep breath. Visualize rocking those babies at the orphanage. They need you, Meredith. I need you. Together we can make this a better world. Trust me. Just this once."

This time she lunged for his hand and felt it close around her wrist. With the sudden movement, her feet slipped off the ledge and her body dangled in the wind with nothing but his grip keeping her from a painful death on the jagged rocks below. She glanced up at his face, barely visible through the pounding rain, and thought she saw him smile.

In that moment, Meredith realized this wasn't what she'd planned in the way of adventure or an escape to a new life. With the newfound determination, she used her free hand to catch hold of his arm.

What was she thinking coming here? In that perilous moment, she remembered.

~ ~ ~ ~

Three weeks earlier

Meredith gripped the armrests of the small engine plane carrying ten passengers. It bounced again, causing her to gasp.

"Almost out of the turbulence, folks. Nothing to worry about. We're beginning our descent. Be sure you're buckled," came the voice over the intercom.

She fussed with her already fastened seat belt. She tried to tighten it farther, without success. A nun sitting next to her had been praying and saying her rosary for a half hour. The last turbulence bump caused the nun to yelp then slam her hand down onto Meredith's leg with the grip of a champion wrestler. The name of Jesus slipped out several times, but she was pretty sure it was a plea to be saved from a watery death over the Caribbean Sea. Meredith patted the woman's hand, more to calm herself down than the good sister.

The plane landed outside the small mountain community of Turtle Bay, that edged the sea, without incident after leaving Phillip Goldson International Airport. Six others disembarked, looking as if they'd been working on a tan rather than going to work every day like herself. The honeymooners pawed at each other at every opportunity and carried Gucci bags. She was maybe twenty years younger than the guy whose taut skin around his mouth and eyes announced he'd had work done on his face. His hands and arms hinted at his true age in spite of the firmness.

"Hope he has a prenup," the sister said softly, elbowing Meredith.

"That's not all he better have," she added, making the sister laugh out loud. "That was inappropriate, Sister Elena. I'm sorry."

"No matter." She waved her off as she struggled to rise from her seat and wiggle out into the aisle. By the time she'd accomplished the act, she laid her hand on her heart and took deep breaths.

"Are you okay, Sister?" Meredith retrieved her backpack from the overhead bin and slung it onto her shoulders. "Let me get your things." She pulled down a small canvas bag, hearing it squeak when she lowered it to the seat.

The sister smiled. "It's toys for the children. My orphanage needs so many things." She tried to take it from Meredith who pulled it back in refusal. "Thank you, dear. This flight was exhausting."

Meredith secured a wheelchair for Sister Elena and rolled her through the small airport to find their luggage. Since the facility boasted only one luggage carousel, it wasn't difficult to locate. She heard an uproar of squeals and laughter, along with calls of Sister Elena's name. Then, like a swarm of grasshoppers, children were hugging and kissing the sister, talking ninety miles an hour until she held up her hand for silence. Some squatted next to her, and a few others patted her arm. The rest stood back and waited.

"My goodness. I have missed you little rascals. Now, where is your escort?"

"Here I am," called a deep voice. A man strolled up next to her and picked up a little boy no more than three years old. "The bus is waiting. They insisted on coming, Sister Elena. I made them promise not to tire you out."

Meredith gazed at the man before her, dressed in ripped jeans and a faded green T-shirt most likely rescued from a thrift store, given how faded and worn it appeared. It hugged his chest, exposing a muscular frame. The sleeves of the outer shirt were frayed and rolled up high enough, tattoos were visible.

"Thank you again for all your help today and for making me laugh." The sister grinned up at her and reached for her hands, which Meredith gladly gave the sweet old lady. The sister turned to the children then to the man holding the little boy. "Meredith Marshall meet Axel Cahill. She is a nurse practitioner from Missouri.

Axel is also from Missouri."

"Really?" she said, feeling a wave of awkwardness as if he had just noticed her, although with his dark sunglasses, she couldn't be sure. From what she could determine by the straight line of his full lips, and the chin-up motion of greeting, he wasn't a big talker.

The children became impatient as Sister Elena pointed to her one piece of luggage with several pieces of duct tape used as patches. Meredith rushed to grab it at the same time Axel put his hand over hers and pulled the suitcase free. In spite of having a three-year-old clinging to his back, he managed to lift the heavy suitcase before making eye contact with her.

"I got it. Thanks."

Meredith couldn't decide if his tone was condescending, impatient, or bored. Either way, he turned away from her as she scrambled to pull her luggage off the carousel. She dropped one piece, and it popped open, spilling underwear, bras, cosmetics, and a couple of bikinis onto the circling carousel, headed to return inside the secret place of all lost luggage.

"No. No. No," she cried as she tried to gather up a few pieces. At one point, she reached too far over and fell face-first into her open suitcase. Her legs were kicking up in the air as she tried to right herself, only to catch the front of her shirt on something sharp that ripped a hole over one breast. Since her bra now was visible to God and everyone else in Belize, she placed her hand over the front as she shoved with the other hand to return to the floor.

Hearing the children cheer, she watched Axel step onto the carousel, taking long strides until he jammed Sister Elena's cane into the mechanical works. It vibrated then groaned to a stop. Unconcerned, he proceeded to bend down and gather up the remaining pieces of clothing. He lifted her black lacy bra with one finger then turned to eye her head to toe.

Maintaining his solemn expression, he tossed it to her, and it landed on her head. "Nice," was all he said then shoved the rest of what was now vacation debris into her suitcase and hopped to the floor. He carried it to a nearby table where a bucket of what appeared to be school supplies was stored. With the speed of Wile E. Coyote, he duct taped the suitcase shut then placed it on the floor.

She stood there with her mouth open, the heat of embarrassment painted on her face, holding the lacy bra across the front of her ripped blouse. Realizing the children were giggling at her and the other tourists were smirking, Meredith shoved the bra into her backpack.

"Thank you," she managed to tell him.

He nodded, picked up Sister Elena's suitcase, and made a path through the excited children. One of the older children positioned himself to push the wheelchair as they headed for the exit when she heard Sister Elena call to her.

"Come with us." She motioned. "We'll drop you off at your hotel. It isn't far. There are only three in town. The others are big resorts down the beach." She looked at Axel. "We have room for one more?"

"Anything you want, Sister." For Sister Elena, he offered a warm smile. He bent down, and she put both her tiny hands on his cheeks, causing him to chuckle. He kissed her forehead then turned to Meredith, the gruffness back in his voice. Before she could resist, he snatched her suitcase from her hand. Like a choregraphed dance, everyone moved to the outside, where a small yellow school bus with St. Francis Children's Home scribbled in black letters waited for them. It resembled something a small child could have written. There were abstract flowers painted on the side, and each wheel was a different color.

Watching Axel help Sister Elena into the bus impressed her that maybe he wasn't the creepy homeless guy he appeared to imitate. Once she was settled, the children rushed on, some sitting three in a seat. A little black-haired girl who held hands with the little boy Axel held earlier came to sit by her. It was clear they were twins. Since it was a tight squeeze, she held her arms out for the little girl, who quickly climbed into her lap. The boy smiled up at her and talked so fast, Meredith could only chuckle.

The motion of the bus, stopping and jerking as if it were about to quit, caused her to feel a wave of motion sickness. Combined with the heat and lack of air-conditioning, she hoped throwing up wouldn't add to her already compromised appearance. She managed to pull out a tank top from her backpack to pull over her ripped blouse. When the brakes squeaked to a halt and black exhaust belched like a shotgun blast, Axel opened the door and nodded for her to follow.

Sitting the little one down in the seat, she tousled her hair and added a light pinch to their cheeks, causing them to smother their giggles with a hand across their mouths. The children sang as Sister Elena waved her finger in the air, like a baton at a choral concert. Meredith backed down the aisle, listening and dragging her suitcase with a missing wheel. The music sounded heavenly, until she bumped against a hard body behind her.

With a quick pivot, she caught her toe on the seat leg and fell into the chest of Axel, who stood like a statue glaring down at her with a frown and raised eyebrows. She became aware that her arm had gone around his waist. "Oh. Sorry."

"Were you drinking on the plane?" he asked offhandedly.

"Most certainly not," she snapped, trying to withdraw her arm, only to realize her watch had snagged his T-shirt underneath his open shirt. "Oh no," she said once more and dropped her hold on the suitcase, hoping to free herself of his shirt. He allowed her to try patiently, only to make a bigger mess by tugging a thread loose that unraveled to about two feet as she tried to shake it free.

Finally, he lifted her hand to his mouth and bit off the thread then dropped her hand. He reached for her suitcase and nodded toward the stepdown on the bus. "I've got this. Go before you hurt yourself."

Mortified, Meredith could only nod and start down the two steps, but Sister Elena reached out from the front seat and took her arm. "Axel will return for you tonight. Dinner is at six." She opened her mouth to protest, but the sister's face lit up with such hope as the children cheered her on.

"Thank you. I look forward to it."

The hotel was far from glamorous or modern in appearance. However, it had all the old-world charm of the once British colony she imagined. Large pots with palms, furniture made of rattan with brightly colored cushions, shuttered windows that managed to let tons of light in to cast shadows across the mosaic floor. It was clean, which was her top priority right now. The reviews had been five stars, for the most part. There was even a small swimming pool and office services. She had noticed on the brochure she'd secured, internet was available for an additional fee added to your bill. That was the last thing she wanted here. The whole idea was to escape.

Axel set her suitcase down and motioned for a young bellhop, and gave him some bills from his pocket before he spoke. "Take this lady's luggage to her room while she checks in."

"Thanks, Axel. Business has been slow today."

Both men nodded then fist-bumped. She doubted after the first impression she'd displayed for him, there would be a fist bump for her. He removed his sunglasses, revealing blue eyes and a few crow's feet beginning to form. The blond stubble along his jawline gave him a rugged vibe, one Meredith found startling. His tanned skin on his face and muscled arms gave her a sense of regret she hadn't given a better impression.

What was she thinking? The whole reason she came to this out-of-the-way part of the world was to leave the familiar and a man who made her swear "never again." Maybe she should become a nun. Yet, looking at Axel's blond hair that fell to his shoulders, twisted and tangled from the tropical breezes, she couldn't help but wonder if he had been some kind of Special Forces guy or a cover model for a romance novel. The handmade cord bracelets on both wrists were various colors and gave her the impression that perhaps the children had made them for him. She figured he could wear a dirty sock around his neck and make it stylish.

"Check-in is over there. Everyone is very helpful. If

you need anything, just ask," he said, turning to leave then seeming to think better of it and faced her again. "Thanks for helping Sister Elena."

"She is a jewel. And thank you for helping me." Seriously, she thought, I'm trying desperately to be pleasant and not a total clumsy clown, even if you are a bit rude.

Axel lifted his chin in acceptance of her thank-you then replaced the sunglasses on his nose, waved at a couple of hotel employees, and disappeared through the open front doors.

CHAPTER 2

Axel navigated his motorcycle down the narrow streets of what the locals called Turtle Bay. He loved it here, away from the bright lights of Los Angeles or wherever his contract forced him to go. The air was clean, the water clear, and the people genuine. They didn't have much, but what they had was everything for a good life. It remained his refuge away from the world where he didn't belong.

Few tourists came here. No resorts or high-dollar things to do like parasailing, or snorkeling over the second largest reef in the world. People who came here wanted the tropical rainforest experience, breezes that chased away whatever burdens they carried, and warm sand pushing between their toes as they watched the next generation of baby sea turtles escape to the clear blue waters of the Caribbean Sea.

So, why then did Meredith Marshall come here? She had the appearance of someone who had money: pretty skin, silky auburn hair with a few blonde highlights, and the body of a runway model. The helpless expression in her dark-brown eyes at the airport confused him as to if he should laugh at her predicament or reassure her no one noticed. This woman was definitely out of her element. Even though the luggage appeared old, the designer label spoke loud and clear. The only thing that impressed him was her kindness to Sister Elena and the children. Now he had to fetch her, so he opted not to take the Jeep he left parked at the orphanage in case of emergencies. Instead, he chose to take the motorcycle, confident she'd be uncomfortable and irritated by the time they arrived back there.

He strode into the lobby of the hotel and toward the desk to ask for Meredith. The clerk smiled sheepishly and pointed behind him. As he turned, a young woman approached from the dimness of the area near the windows. The out-of-sorts woman he'd left several hours earlier had transformed into a lovely creature who appeared to fit in to these surroundings. Her hair fell down past her shoulders, still a bit damp and curled on the ends. The turquoise tank top and brown wrap skirt accented her slender body enough that several men in the lobby now stared after her.

"You seem a little more relaxed," he managed to say as she joined him, slinging her purse over her shoulder. "Ready to go?"

"I feel like I need to get something to take. Could we stop at a store?"

"Sure." He led her to the curb where his bike was parked then took advantage of the moment and eyed her legs and sandals. "Guess I should have brought the car."

"No problem. I've done this before." She lifted her

skirt and straddled the back, and he settled in front of her. He couldn't help but grin as he turned the key in the ignition.

He helped her off the bike at the grocery store and watched her run inside. She had a youthful energy he liked, in spite of himself. He didn't generally like tourists because they seemed to think being in Belize gave them the same privilege they enjoyed in the States or wherever they came from. If you stayed here, then you better be prepared for the basics and local cuisine. Meredith was turning out to be different, he decided, as she joined him carrying a small brown paper bag. She held it up.

"I bought peppermint for the children. Hope I got enough. Might need you to bring me back if I run out." She slipped on the back without help. He couldn't help but eye her in suspicion, as he slowly joined her. "It's all right, isn't it? I mean, I wouldn't want to break any rules."

Her arm went around his midriff, and he laid a hand on hers for some reason then removed it. "You strike me as a woman who likes to break rules. Why else would you come to a place like this?" He turned his head slightly to see if she would respond. What he got was a cautious and solemn expression that spoke volumes.

Maybe he drove too fast and that caused her to tighten her hold on his body, but whatever it was, he decided it wasn't totally unpleasant. He slowed to tell her about a few points of interest then sped up again. She leaned in closer to hear him, and her hair touched his face before she captured it and pushed it back. But she remained quiet, nodding when he pointed at something and attentive to her surroundings.

When they reached the orphanage, he quickly dismounted and assisted his passenger once more. She pushed her hair away from her face. The once-tame locks were now windblown and tangled with out-of-control curls. The fresh face appeared calm and unperturbed that her appearance had taken on a wild, enticing aura he found interesting. She sucked in a long breath and then released it suddenly.

"That was some ride. Do you always drive like a bat out of hell?"

"Always."

"Guess you're a rule breaker, too."

"Every chance I get."

"I figured as much. I'll walk back to the hotel after dinner."

"It's a long walk."

"You took several detours and ran two stop signs. I'm guessing you thought those speed limit signs were just suggestions. I'm probably a block and a half away from the hotel."

"The store wasn't exactly on the way."

"No candy for you tonight."

"I wouldn't be so sure of that, Miss High and Mighty," he mumbled as she turned and walked up the four steps. With her head held high, shoulders back, she continued to push her hair from her face when the breezes teased the long strands. He couldn't help but stare after her; there was something about the woman that made him curious as to who she was.

~ ~ ~ ~

Meredith could feel his eyes on her. What a sketchy, disrespectful jerk. That once-over he gave her was far from a friendly observation. She fully expected him to salivate on the street, like some werewolf that would cause them to take a slide into a flower cart. Men. Why couldn't they just be normal humans who cared about climate change instead of their next conquest?

There remained something familiar about him. Maybe it was his flippant attitude or his rough-and-tumble appearance, like he didn't care what anyone thought of him. That certainly struck a chord in her. She refused to consider she merely found him attractive in spite of mismatched clothes and tattoos. The confident air he waved like a flag only managed to remind her of how fragile her life was right now. The fear and suspicion of everything and everyone continued to plague her.

Seeing that kissy-face couple from the plane in the grocery store gave her pause. Why would Mr. Moneybags and Trophy Wife be shopping? And why didn't they take a shuttle to the resort instead of staying at the tiny boutique hotel she chose? Considering the rock on her finger, Trophy Wife didn't strike her as a person who liked shabby chic hotels with little air-conditioning and no room service.

Were they following her? Who were they really? She shook it off. Paranoia turned out to be her constant companion since the divorce.

"Meredith," Sister Elena called as she entered the orphanage. "Come. Come. The children are anxious to show you around."

The large rooms, cooled by ceiling fans and open windows with screens attached, were welcoming. Her sandals clicked on tile floors as she walked. Sister Elena was barefoot, so she removed her shoes, too, and placed them by the door where Axel placed his.

"I hope it was okay I brought treats for the children," she said, handing the sister the small brown sack. "If not, then feel free to toss it."

Sister Elena peeked inside and smiled. "I should save this for Christmas, but they will love the surprise." She waved Axel to come forward and quickly received a hug. Patting his cheek, he lowered his face so she could kiss him on each side of his face. "Such a good boy."

He grinned like a little boy as he lifted those blue eyes to Meredith then glanced away. Definitely the devil in blue jeans. The thought of him being some kind of shape shifter also popped into her head. One minute, a sweet angel who protected small children, the next, a rogue warrior with a forked tail and horns who devoured innocent women who dared visit his part of the world.

Before she could start a mental list of why she didn't trust this guardian angel of the orphanage, a thunderous stampede of little feet entered the room, their laughter bouncing off the high ceiling. They circled her; one she scooped up in her arms, the others either patting her and talking all at once or pulling her forward to see their home. There was nothing to do but join in the merriment and be surprised at each word they spoke.

Such happiness had eluded her for too long. It almost hurt to laugh and smile like this. Each child wanted to show her their room. The boys were in one dormitory-style room and the girls in a similar one. It was crowded with five girls and six boys.

"I want to stay with my brother," the little twin girl said as she pointed to her brother turning her attention to Meredith. She set her bare feet down next to her brother then kneeled next to them. Both wrapped their arms around her neck then laid their heads on her shoulder. "Would you be our mommy?"

"Then we could be together," the little boy said happily and added a tight hug.

"Run along, children," Sister Elena said. "Help the others set the table. Dinner is almost ready." Sister Elena handed Meredith a tissue from her pocket then rushed toward a call from the kitchen.

An open hand appeared in front of her face, causing her to glance up at Axel. His expression had softened and he'd swapped the devil persona for the angel one. She slipped her hand into his so he could pull her up from her awkward position on the floor. One more dab at her eyes then she slipped the tissue into her pocket. She had a feeling it wouldn't be the last time it would be needed.

"Do you have kids?" he asked, stepping back.

"No. My ex didn't want kids. One of my biggest regrets."

"Me, too," he admitted. There was something in his voice that drew her attention to his face. His eyes narrowed as he observed the children dance away into other parts of the house they called home. "They can beat you up with their laughter, and especially their stories."

She joined him as he moved toward the dining room. "Looks like the place could use some updating."

"I've done what I can. Supplies and mostly workers can be tough to get. They make more in the tourist industry."

"So, that's your job here? Handyman?" she asked casually. "I imagine that is a steady income for you, at least." She sounded pleased. "I bet, with so many little ones, there is always something to fix."

He nodded and boxed with a little boy of about eight. Clearly, he let him sneak a punch to the gut and bent over in fake pain.

Meredith reminded herself not to be tricked into liking him, no matter if he boxed and lost to every child in the orphanage. He was trouble. She could almost smell it. Or was that eucalyptus oil? She loved eucalyptus and often wore it to bed at night to help her sleep. Stealing a sideways glance at the too-good-to-be-true handyman with the tattoos and muscles, she decided the two-day stubble on his face and long blond hair must be a lonely woman trap. No thanks. Catching sight of Sister Elena, she hurried toward safety.

"Sister Elena, let me help with something. I'm used to being busy."

"Well, there is something you could do for us, maybe tomorrow, if you have time." She gave her a timid, sheepish expression. "We talked on the plane about you being a pediatric nurse practitioner. We can't really afford checkups for the children, and some of these little monkeys have never been to the doctor."

"I would be happy to check them out, Sister. What about vaccinations?"

"No money for that, either. We are a charity"—she grinned—"with not many charitable funds coming in." The nun rolled her eyes skyward and put her hands together like she might pray. "God sent you to us."

Meredith couldn't help but chuckle as she turned and saw Axel leaning against the doorframe with his arms folded across his chest. His smirk gave her goose bumps as she evaluated the situation. Maybe God did send her here to help and to heal her tired soul, but the devil sent his helper to wreak a little havoc in her common sense.

CHAPTER 3

The children, no matter how small, each had a job to do after dinner. The cook, Luis, a stout man with chubby cheeks and a dirty apron, joined them for the meal. He was a jovial man who wore a cross around his neck, offered grace before they ate, and promised the children a story afterward if they ate all their food.

The twins sat on each side of her and asked her questions ranging from where she was from to how much she weighed. Most of their inquiries made her laugh and led her to make up an outlandish response causing shock or gasps from the twins.

"You children let Ms. Meredith eat in peace," Sister Elena scolded but still managed to let one corner of her mouth lift in a teasing fashion. She followed up by pointing her fork at Axel at the far end of the table. "Axel, Luis and I will get the children bathed and ready for bed tonight. Would you please give Meredith a tour of our little clinic?"

He cut his eyes toward her before tilting his head.

"She's on vacation, Sister. I doubt she wants to see our clinic."

"You have a clinic? Sister, you didn't tell me it was finished." Meredith forced herself to avoid making eye contact with the man. His expressionless face made him too hard to read for her liking. "I would love to see it. But I'm happy to wait for you, Sister Elena. I can come back tomorrow. My schedule is wide open. I'm here to relax, do a little reading, and see the sea turtles, of course."

Sister Elena opened her mouth as if she might protest when Axel rose from his seat while wiping his face with a cloth napkin. "Sounds like a better idea," he said flatly before nodding to Luis. "I'll take a look at that washing machine for you now before I take our guest"—he cut his eyes back to her like he might turn on the lasers to slice off her head—"back to the hotel. Let me know when you're ready."

"Thank you." She plastered a fake smile on her lips, knowing full well he would detect her insincerity.

He raised his chin and stared down his nose at her like she was akin to a cockroach.

"Sister, may I help with the children?" She laid her hand on her heart. "I will even tell them some stories or read to them if Luis needs to help Axel. They've all cleaned their plates, which is no surprise considering how delicious everything tasted."

Luis beamed and stood to join Axel. "Thank you, Ms. Meredith. But I'm not sure…" he teased. When the children cheered at her suggestion and looked at Luis to agree, he winked good-naturedly. "Okay. But if they give you any trouble, let me know."

When they wiggled and cheered, she clapped her

hands and cheered, too. This seemed to soften Axel's expressionless face before he disappeared into another room.

Realizing how tired the sister must be after such a long day of travel and returning home, Meredith made an extra effort to do whatever task needed to be attended to, especially when she noticed the sister struggling. Fortunately, the sister didn't need much persuasion to sit down and let her tuck in the children after teeth were brushed and a story read to them. Bedtime prayers followed with the twins Rosa and Pedro giving thanks for Ms. Meredith. When she finished tucking the last child in, Rosa had disappeared.

"My guess is Pedro has escaped as well," the sister sighed. "They like for Axel to tell them good night. I'm sure time has slipped away for him. Would you mind going to get them while I turn out the lights?"

Meredith was headed down the stairs and through the kitchen when she heard voices in the room at the back of the house. Walking in, she found Luis rinsing his hands and Axel sitting on the floor trying to work on the washing machine. Luis said, "It's on its last leg, Axel. I don't know if you can put it together one more time. The dryer is next."

"I'll buy a new one when I get my next check. No worries," he responded calmly as he grimaced then turned his wrench to tighten a trouble area on something she couldn't see. "This should hold it."

The little boy, Pedro, nodded and repeated, "Yep. That should hold it." He stood behind him and patted the now-bare shoulder of the handyman. His twin, Rosa, stood on the other side and twisted her fingers absentmindedly through his shoulder-length hair. Part of it had been pulled back in a ponytail to keep out of his eyes.

She couldn't help admire the scene. Besides possessing a fine chiseled body that reminded her of a bad boy, most likely with a criminal past, the kindness that showed in his eyes as he turned to look at the boy touched her heart. A tattoo etched across both shoulders resembled a Celtic knot. Rosa dropped her little hand to the tattoo and traced it, causing him to shiver.

"Stop it, you little monkey," he snapped angrily which only caused her to refuse and trace it again. Pedro laughed now and did the same. "That's it," he declared and managed to jump to his feet. He spotted her when he was halfway through a playful reprimand.

"Sister Elena told me to come get the children for bed." Rosa ran to her and she quickly lifted her little body up into her arms. Pedro came and hugged her legs. "I can't pick up both of you, Pedro, but if you wait here, I'll come back for you."

"How about I take you, Pedro?" Axel asked as he wiped his hands on a nearby towel.

The little boy jumped up and down with delight when Rosa put both her hands on Meredith's cheeks. "You should be our mommy. So pretty." Rosa wrinkled her button nose at Axel who stepped up beside her then picked up Pedro. "And you could be our daddy, Axel."

She waited for him to growl a response, but he reached out and pinched the little girl's cheek. "I think Ms. Meredith is way too fancy for my way of life, little one. But you're right. She is kinda pretty." He locked onto her surprised glance and gave her one of those smirks that made her understand that Little Red Riding Hood fell for the wolf's line of baloney because she was probably in love with him. "That's enough of your silliness for one day. Come on. You guys need to go to bed."

By the\ time they reached the top of the stairs, the twins had laid their heads on adult shoulders. Just before they separated, the twins reached out and took each other's hand and whispered, "I love you."

"See you in the morning, sissy," Pedro said. Still holding his hand, Rosa kissed it.

After tucking the children in, Meredith exited with her head down, sniffing back tears. She ran into Axel's chest, jumped, momentarily terrified, and fell back against the wall. The rapid heartbeat caused her to hyperventilate, remembering the last time she'd run into a male brick wall.

Axel stepped back and reached a hand out, which only made her side step him.

"I'm sorry. I didn't mean to startle you," he said slowly. Eyeing her with concern, he arched an eyebrow. "Are you all right?"

Meredith straightened herself with an internal shake to control the fear of being surprised by a man. "Yes. I'm fine. I should go."

"I'll get the car."

"I'll walk. Thanks." She hurried down the steps and found Sister Elena sitting on the front porch in a swing, fanning herself. "Everyone is tucked in, Sister. I'll be going. I'll drop by tomorrow to visit the clinic."

Luis strolled out and nodded to the nun then to Meredith. "Leaving so soon? Your hotel is several blocks away. Let me call Axel to take you back."

"No. I need to walk. I think it is well lit and there are still lots of people moving about. I'll be fine."

A Jeep screeched to a stop in front of the orphanage, and Axel motioned for her. "Come on. It's on my way."

"Such a good boy." Sister Elena beamed toward where Axel parked. "Go on, Meredith. We'll talk tomorrow."

Timidly, she walked down the steps toward the Jeep. Once inside, he drove like a respectable human being. He didn't try to engage in conversation on the way back to the hotel. Pulling into a parking spot, he jumped out and offered a hand as she tried to maneuver her way out.

"I'll walk you in."

"No need."

"Sister Elena would pull me across the room by my ear if I didn't. It's what a gentleman should do." He narrowed his eyes at her with a mixture of curiosity and reserve that somehow made her less suspicious of him.

Meredith nodded and headed toward the front doors, a little less rushed than she planned. He moved alongside her, putting enough space between them as not to make her feel threatened. The twins felt like a safe topic to interact with him.

"Those twins have stolen my heart. What's their story?"

They reached the top step to the open hotel doors when he pointed to a vacant porch swing. Together, they sat down, Axel appearing to put as much distance between them as possible. "Kids get adopted all the time from the orphanage, but Sister Elena has made sure they are a package deal. No one seems to want that."

Meredith couldn't help but lay her hand over her heart as he continued.

"Mother and father died in a boating accident. Not much family to speak of and the parents had written that Sister Elena be guardian until a proper family could be found."

Meredith could feel herself about to make a decision that should be given a great deal of thought instead of, "I want them. What do I have to do to make that happen?"

"Typical. American tourist comes down here and falls in love with the culture and atmosphere then returns home to real life. You can't take these kids away from everything they've ever known. This ain't Disneyland." He stood up. "Get that thought out of your head. A few more days and you'll tire of being manipulated by three-year-olds who have their own set of problems that some fancy, spoiled, do-gooder has no idea how to cope with. Good night, Meredith." He hurried down the steps and, in seconds, she could hear the Jeep roar to life and disappear into the night.

~ ~ ~ ~

Axel returned to the orphanage to find Sister Elena still sitting on the front porch swing. He knew she had to be exhausted. The volunteers who came to spend the night so she could rest would not be coming for a few days because of a family funeral. He planned to put a cot outside the children's rooms and be there if anyone needed attending. You just never knew with kids.

"Sister, you need to go to bed. I'll lock up. It's been a long day for you. Sleep in. I've got you covered."

She stood and let him loop her arm through his. "Such a good boy. Do you like Meredith? Isn't she special?"

"I wouldn't know."

"It is a blessing."

"How did you meet? Just on the plane?"

"Oh no. I met her at the hospital in the children's ward I visited. She is a nurse practitioner. I don't remember if I told you that. She was so kind and helpful to the patients. I invited her to come here and work. She also worked the ER when needed."

"Sister Elena," he groaned. "You can't afford someone like that. And besides, what makes you think she would even want to?"

"I prayed she'd have a change of heart." The sister leaned in to him playfully and pointed to the heavens. "He knows what we need." She slapped Axel's arm as he led her to her room. "She turned me down. But then, as I was waiting in line to board the plane, I spotted her running toward me." She closed her eyes and appeared euphoric. "It was a miracle. She decided to come to see our little operation here after all."

"Didn't that strike you a little odd?" He sighed. "You're too trusting. What do you know about this woman?"

"Nothing." She waved him off as she entered her room. "Now you be nice to her. I want her to stay. The children seem to like her. And the twins have already told me they want her to be their mommy. Maybe it will happen." She closed her door.

"Over my dead body," he mumbled and walked away. He pulled out his cell phone and dialed. A familiar voice picked up almost immediately. "Hey, it's me, Jake. I need you to check someone out. Can you do that?"

CHAPTER 4

Axel didn't hear back from his friend right away. Removing his shirt and flip-flops, he lay down on his cot outside the dormitory rooms and quickly fell asleep. As daylight began to break, a little hand patted him on the shoulder, waking him from a sound sleep. He hadn't realized how tired he was until his head hit the pillow.

While Sister Elena had gone to the States to raise money for the orphanage and speak at a conference, he and Luis had taken charge. They managed the staff and pitched in where needed, and there was always extra things to be done, like grocery shopping, lessons, and repairs.

"Rosa," he said, swinging his legs to the floor.

"I don't feel good." She sniffed.

He felt her head. She was burning up. Lifting her into his arms, he headed downstairs. "Sister," he yelled, knowing she was a little hard of hearing and a sound sleeper. "Sister," he called again. This time, she came to the door, yawning and rubbing her eyes. Before she could respond to his call, he reached for her hand and laid it on Rosa's forehead. "She's on fire."

Concern filled her eyes as she took the child from his arms. "Get me some cool, wet washcloths for her head then go get Meredith." He stared at her for a second too long before she snapped like a hungry crocodile, "Do it now, Axel."

There were a lot of things he knew how to do: repair washing machines, survive in the wilderness with nothing but a pocket knife and a piece of twine, take out an enemy silently before they knew he was even there, and a lot of other things that would mark him as a dangerous man, but holding a sick little girl left him helpless and afraid.

He called Luis to come early before he checked on the other children still sound asleep. The sun was rising as he hopped into the Jeep and headed for the hotel. Screeching to a halt in the front without bothering to find a parking spot, he rushed up the steps and into the lobby.

"I need to find Meredith Marshall's room," he told the young clerk at the desk. "What room?"

"I can't tell you that, Axel. Against hotel policy."

"Sister Elena is asking for her. We need help with a sick child. She's a nurse or something."

"I don't know…" He hesitated.

Axel reached across the counter, grabbed him by the collar, and pulled him across to be nose to nose. "Now."

"L-let me check," he stuttered. In seconds, he had written down the room number on a piece of paper, which Axel snatched from his fingers. "I'll call first."

"You do that," he growled as he stormed down the

hall.

Luckily, she was on the first floor. By the time he got to her room, she was opening the door. Fear was in her eyes as he pushed inside. She jumped back and tried to put distance between them.

"Rosa is sick. Sister said you could help. She's burning up." In a blink of an eye, her expression turned from fear to acceptance. He noticed in that moment she stood in nothing but a thin camisole and boxers. "How soon can you be ready?" He couldn't help but stare at her. She was beautiful in the morning light coming through the shutters. Tangled auburn hair around her shoulders and slim limbs gave him a feeling long missing in his life.

"A few minutes. Can you grab my backpack? I have supplies in there." She was already pulling on a pair of capris over the boxers. When she turned to go into the bathroom, he spotted bruises across her shoulders and down her back. "The backpack is over there." She pointed then grabbed a T-shirt off the chair.

Unlike a lot of women he'd known, one in particular, it really did take less than a minute for her to return. She was tying her hair up in a messy bun when she walked out of the bathroom and had slipped into a scooped-neck coral-colored T-shirt. "I'm good to go. Did you find the bag?" She moved toward him.

"I got it. Let's go. You can tell me what you need once we get there, and I'll make a run to the pharmacy." He slung the backpack over one shoulder and opened the door for her. "I'm parked out front."

It seemed like only seconds had passed when she buckled herself in and grabbed the framing around the door as he turned the key. Even though he drove too fast, Meredith didn't complain. When he pulled up outside the orphanage, she grabbed her backpack and ran up the steps without him. Maybe she did care. Maybe she was the real deal. He wished his friend had gotten back to him before he ran like a crazy person to get her help. What if she were an imposter?

He returned the Jeep to the garage before heading back inside. Voices were coming from a spare room next to Sister Elena's. When he walked in, Meredith held Rosa who was crying.

"Rosa, my love, I'm going to see what's wrong, okay? Does anything hurt?"

She nodded as huge tears rolled down her red cheeks. She pointed to her tummy.

"Come on. Lie down here," she said, trying to pull her arms from around her neck. When she refused and clung to her even tighter, Axel stepped up and removed her grip.

"Rosa, I'm here, too. Be a good girl for me and do what Meredith tells you. Please," he said with a weak smile. When she jutted out her bottom lip and nodded her head in agreement, Axel took her and laid her on the twin bed. "That's my girl."

Meredith had a medical kit in her backpack, along with a stethoscope. She checked her temperature then her lungs before using the otoscope to examine her ears. "Do you have any Children's Tylenol, Sister Elena?"

She nodded and scurried off to get it.

"It's okay, sweetie. I'm going to make you better."

Just then her twin stumbled in, pulling at his ear. "I don't feel good."

"Bring him here, Axel. He's probably got the same thing. It isn't uncommon for twins to get sick at the same time with the same ailment."

Sister Elena returned with water and the medicine. Both children got a dose for fever and pain. Twenty minutes later, they were dozing off with their hands locked together.

"They look like little angels," Sister sighed. "Thank you, Meredith. What is wrong with them?"

"They have an ear infection, which explains the fever. Their lungs are clear. Not sure about their stomach ache but, if you have a lab, I might be able to run a test. In the meantime, I'd like to give them an antibiotic. Do you have any in the clinic?"

Sister Elena shook her head.

"Axel, I'll write a prescription for each of them. Will that be a problem, or can you get it filled? I can go with you and show my credentials."

"No need. He owes me. Make a list of anything else you need."

"The staff should be here soon to help out." Sister Elena brushed the children's hair from their faces.

"When they get here, I want all the beds stripped and linens and blankets washed in case there is some kind of germ going around."

"Like what?" Axel asked.

"Although their throats were slightly inflamed, it might be nothing. However, the symptoms of strep throat include sore throat, fever, and abdominal pain. Add an ear infection, and the twins could be very contagious."

"Sounds serious," Sister Elena said, rubbing her hands nervously.

"Well, it can be, if not treated. Ear infections are common with little ones. Something to watch out for in the future." She rubbed the sister's arm. "I've seen this a lot, Sister Elena. If I think my treatment isn't working, I'll know by this evening. At that point, I'll have Axel drive me to the nearest hospital in Belize City. Okay?"

"Okay," she said, fighting back tears.

"After breakfast, I'll go to your clinic and check each child. If you have records, I'd like to see them. I will record any and all information I find, along with any treatment I suggest. Will that be acceptable to you, Sister?"

"Certainly."

"Axel? Is that okay with you?"

He felt like a nervous father and appreciated Meredith asking his permission, considering he'd been a jerk to her. There was still doubt gnawing at his brain, but he managed to nod in agreement.

"Great. And when the helpers get here, your room needs to be sanitized, Sister. I will check you out in the clinic, too. Can't have the most important person here be sick and grouchy like your handyman over there."

She looked his way and the corners of her mouth lifted. At least she remained calm doing her job. "You going to check me out, too?" he quipped.

"If I can give you a shot in the hip for whatever it is you take to be such a pain in the neck." She cut her eyes to the sister, who snickered under the hand she placed over her mouth. "I'll be a minute, Axel. Sorry. I know you're worried about them. I will do my best. I'll go make a list of some basic things that might help them feel better. Sister, you can check my list and cross out anything you already have."

Axel watched her go into the other room to find

paper and pencil before turning to check on the twins. "I feel helpless," he said softly. "Hope she knows what she's doing."

"Why are you so worried? I saw her working at a children's hospital myself. And I saw the way you couldn't take your eyes off her when you thought no one would notice." She shook her finger at him and winked. "You like her."

"No. I'm suspicious. Something doesn't add up."

"Don't you scare her off, Axel. We need her here in our clinic. I'm getting too old to worry about such things."

He threw up his hands in frustration and turned away as his phone vibrated. "I have to take this." Walking out into the corridor, he spotted Meredith sitting at the dining room table, scribbling her list. He moved outside onto the front porch and sat in the swing where he could see through the house and if she searched for him. "Yeah. What ya got for me, Jake?"

"Not much, but enough to know the woman is on the run. She resigned her position at a children's hospital under suspicious circumstances the day Sister Elena met her. Everyone seemed surprised, since she was well liked and respected. There was a three-week gap until the sister flew home. There's no indication they met again. Her divorce was final a month before that."

"The reason for the divorce?"

"Don't know. She was seen in the ER following the decree. Apparently, the ex wasn't happy about the arrangement. She had a restraining order against him. He has a gambling problem and is in over his head in debt. Lost the house, new cars, maybe his job. He's a lawyer for some big firm. Was on track to be partner."

"And now?"

"Not sure, but he's driving a ten-year-old used car and staying in a rental."

"Sounds like you know more about him than her. No wonder she left. I saw bruises on her back and shoulders."

"Yeah. The divorce was a long time coming, I think. They've been separated a couple of years. On again-off again kind of thing. As I said earlier, she was well respected at the hospital. Several long-time friends outside of work tried to get in touch with her, and, when they couldn't, they feared the worst. Apparently, they filed a missing person's report. The report indicated when she left the ER the last time—"

"Last time?"

"Right. The friends indicated the ex-husband brought her to the ER a year earlier. Said she twisted her ankle, fell, and broke her wrist. The friends took turns staying with her for a while." There was the crinkle of paper moving on the other end of the phone, as if Jake might be checking his notes.

Axel felt his temper rise in his chest. "Sorry. Didn't mean to interrupt. You were saying?"

"Anyway, she came into the ER alone the last time. The girlfriends reported she had been spooked about something. They didn't know what because she kept brushing them off."

"Why did she come in the last time?"

"Probably for the bruises you saw. The hospital ER took good care of her and wanted to call the police, but she said she'd just call friends to pick her up. The hospital staff were concerned when a couple of thugs showed up."

"Thugs?"

"The Russian kind. No mistaking the accent. They stuck to her like glue. She went willingly and, apparently, they weren't exactly strangers. Paid her bill and asked for instructions on her care. When the hospital called to follow up on her, she was gone."

"Running with the mob. Great. They could follow her here."

"Paid for her plane ticket with cash. At least the first one she took. All her credit cards canceled. As a matter of fact, she has been slowly wiping away her identity for several months. I'll send you the rest."

"To my phone. Nowhere else."

"Done."

"Thanks, buddy."

Clicking off, he spotted Meredith rise from the dining room table and go back into where Sister Elena cared for the children. She studied the list as she stepped out to join him.

"Here you go." She extended her hand with the paper. "Sister said they have none of these things. Hard to believe," she sighed. She handed him some cash. "I have no idea if this is enough. If not, I'll pay you back."

He couldn't believe she thought he didn't have enough to pay for this.

"Oh sorry. You probably don't make much here. I'll go get you some more cash, just in case."

He stood and read over the list in the early morning light. "I think this will do. If not, I'll make him an offer he can't refuse," he said in his best Marlon Brandon impression from The Godfather movie.

She frowned.

Maybe it was a little too close to home. Shoving the

paper in his pants pocket, he rushed down the steps. "Later."

CHAPTER 5

The volunteers and paid helpers showed up soon after Axel left. Luis got breakfast on the table as the children came down the stairs yawning and rubbing their eyes. They wore their pj's and spoke in mumbles if at all. When they crawled into their chairs, sleepy-eyed and hair going in all directions, she couldn't help but feel happy. She walked around the table, touching each child casually to spot any higher-than-normal temperatures so she could isolate the child.

Luis brought her an apron with faded tropical flowers when he spotted her helping clear the table. She nodded in thanks then went to help the workers strip beds. Checking on the twins to see if they were still sleeping, she found them sitting up, and talking to each other like long-lost friends. Her heart melted when they waved for her to join them.

"Morning, little sea turtles." This made them giggle. Touching their heads, she confirmed they were still warm but not like earlier. "Are you feeling better?" All she got were shrugs.

"You don't look sick to me," called Axel as he walked into the room carrying a pharmacy bag. "Guess I'll have to eat this candy myself."

"No," they called in unison.

"Okay. But only one little piece. First, you have to take the medicine Ms. Meredith tells you to take."

While he fished some candy from his pocket, she accepted the bag and inspected the contents. She took their temperatures again, and they were still both 101 degrees. Their throats were red. Their ears remained a problem, so she hoped the antibiotic would take hold quickly. Next, she served up another dose of liquid fever reducer. She used the rapid strep test on each child, much to their protests and tears. After only a few minutes, both tests were positive.

"Did they have any more of these?"

"Got the last two. They're on backorder. Said they don't sell many."

"Well, with any luck we've isolated the twins soon enough. We've done a lot of cleaning so that should help. The antibiotics will kick in and do the hard work. Within twenty-four hours and no fever, they should be good to go."

She suggested they eat something but, when they refused, Axel got them to drink water, along with some Pedialyte. To her surprise, Sister Elena joined them and insisted Axel give her a tour of their little clinic while she read the twins a story. She promised to have them take another nap.

"It's only ten o'clock," Meredith said, rubbing her face. "It feels much later."

They walked across a breezeway between the orphanage and the clinic.

"Luis said you were a big help with the kids while I was gone. Sorry it took so long for me to get back. They had to call Stateside to check on your information."

"Oh?" she said slowly and with a little too much caution. "Where exactly did they call?"

"The hospital where you worked, I think. Why? Is that a problem?" He thought maybe he'd catch her in a lie about why she wasn't working there any longer.

"No. Curious is all. Wondered how things worked here."

"Hardest part was getting someone to answer the phone," he said, opening the door. "Here we are. Guess the sister told you all about it. Money was donated for the building. Used to be a dentist/liquor store. Kind of worked out since most of the time the doctor didn't have enough Novocain to give his patients when he had to pull a tooth." He chuckled. "Anyway, a local went away to school to become a dentist at the expense of the whole community. Came back and set up shop a few streets over from your hotel. Nice guy. Reasonable rates, and he actually knows what he's doing. This went up for sale, and some rich guy bought the place then signed it over to the sister."

Meredith flipped on some lights in the clinic that resembled many she'd visited in the states.

"This is nice. Recently remodeled?"

"Yeah. Kind of a community effort. We're on high ground here so, when the hurricanes come in, this place has never flooded. Finished a few months ago. All we need is a doctor. There's a section in the back"—he pointed down the hall—"that can be used for a small hospital someday. Sister Elena has a lot of faith that will happen. But, for now, we would be happy with a doctor."

"Or a nurse practitioner?"

"So it would seem," he said, leading the way for her to peek in the examining rooms.

"You don't approve of me, do you?" Pivoting with a little more speed than she anticipated caused Axel to run into her, slamming her back against a wall. He reached for her, but she flinched as a cry escaped from deep in her throat.

"I'm sorry," he said, taking a quick step back. "I didn't know you were stopping."

She took in the look of confusion on his face that morphed into concern. "No. No. I—didn't, didn't know you were so close. Just surprised me is all." She faked light laughter. "I think I scared you more." It became obvious that wasn't true when his facial expression changed once again, this time to suspicion.

"Tell you what. I'll leave you here to check things out. You'll probably have questions for Sister Elena. Lab is that way. No idea if what you need is there. Then it might be a good time to make a plan to move on when you turn down the job offer."

"What makes you think I'll turn her down?" That feeling of being led to do something she didn't want smothered her instincts, like it had with her husband and his shady friends.

"You're every do-gooder who comes down here wanting to make a difference. Stay a while, help with the sea turtles, feed the hungry, do a medical clinic or whatever your group is into then you leave. It's hard to live here. You don't strike me as a woman who likes to rough it for very long," he said with a voice void of emotion. "Just don't promise those kids something you have no intention of following through on or bring your own problems to clutter up an already chaotic life for Sister Elena."

Before she could say another word, he turned and left, letting the screen door slam behind him. A chill ran over her at his revelation of her or the motives for being here. But he was right about one thing. Since the pharmacy had taken the initiative to investigate her credentials, chances were good someone would be able to track her down now. How long would it be before she had to move on? No way did she want those children to be in danger.

Touching her shoulder where the bruises were finally healing helped her remember how far she'd come and that at least now she held the ticket to independence. Never again would she be beholden to a man to give her joy and fulfillment.

Freedom to do as she pleased meant carving out a life that had felt impossible before, thanks to a group of people who made her an offer she couldn't refuse. Axel had mentioned as much in an offhand remark the night before. For a few seconds, she'd thought he knew her secret instead of quoting The Godfather. Maybe she could even adopt a child. Part of her unhappiness dealt with the fact that her husband, narcissist that he was, had no room for someone who would take her attention from him.

Methodically, she explored each room, cabinet, table, sat in each chair, and dreamed of what it would be like to have her own clinic and make a difference. How wonderful it would be to see children grow and thrive under her care. For now, it was just a dream, an impossible dream with a few loose ends to tie up. Loose ends that could be dangerous for her if she wasn't careful.

Just how long could she last before escape became her only option?

~ ~ ~ ~

The children were playing outside for the most part. It was the weekend, so they had no school bus to catch. Axel often liked to listen to them chatter and play while he fixed the next broken thing in such an old house. It would soon be time for him to take a month to go to his place down the coast and continue with his own projects. There, he would find peace and quiet, plenty of time to meditate and examine his inner soul as to what he wanted to do with his life.

Luis and his two sisters would be working full-time while he was gone. They could use the money, and no one was more dependable. The women would share a room and be on call 24/7. They were young and unmarried. The money would come in handy for their plans to attend college next year.

An older man named George took his place as handyman. He could keep up with things that broke or just fell apart better than him. The children called him Tata Duende. It came from the old Mayan language: Tate meaning grandfather or old and Duende meaning goblin. He was a gentle soul but actually resembled a bald goblin, even to him.

Checking his email on the phone, he saw a message from his buddy with the information on Meredith. Sister Elena was reading to one of the little girls while several other children colored pictures at the dining room table. She lifted her face toward him and smiled as he passed through.

"Got anything for me today, Sister?"

"Could you go check on the twins? They were asleep about thirty minutes ago."

He nodded.

"Where's Meredith?"

"Still at the clinic. You can send the kids for their checkups when she gives you the okay. Can you spare someone to take the kids one by one?"

She nodded.

"I'll go make sure it's locked up when she gets finished. Just give me a call if I'm not back by then. I will make sure everything is in its place when she goes back to the hotel."

The sister went back to reading as he went to find the twins who were still sleeping. He touched their foreheads and was pleased to find them cool. It was impossible to keep from smiling at them with their small arms draped across each other. They were so full of mischief. How many times had he thought about adopting them?

The time he'd approached the subject of children to his fiancée back in LA didn't go well.

"Do you see this body? I've spent a lot of money to get it this way. I don't want to mess it up." She was a movie star with an expensive lifestyle and a need for things. Fortunately, the Hollywood executives didn't mind paying her whatever she wanted to be a part of their films.

"How about adoption?" he'd suggested.

"I travel all the time and so do you," she'd reasoned.

"We aren't the kind of people who have kids." Once more, she had won the argument and used her wiles to seduce him into agreeing. Finally, he'd had enough and left.

Irritated, he let his thoughts drift back in time to the woman who had, in many ways, made him lose sight of what was important. He'd become worldly and out of touch with reality in her beautiful, glittery life where me, me, me was the rule of the day. Loving the limelight nearly killed the man inside of him. The man who'd trained to be in the military, and, damaged by war, took solace in her attention after being a consultant on one of her movies.

With a cup of coffee in hand, he found his way to the front porch swing and sat down to read the email. The first things that popped up were several pictures of Meredith. They resembled something you'd put on a badge. Probably used on her hospital ID. Several more followed that were grainy but clear enough to see that bruises were on her face and arms. It made him sick to his stomach.

The next pictures appeared to have been taken by a security camera. They involved her talking to two men outside what appeared to be the hospital. They dwarfed her in comparison. Rough, stocky, and hard would be a good description. His buddy had even included security footage of them talking, but there was no sound. Next, he opened the updated file of information.

He heard someone clear their throat and looked up from his phone to see Meredith standing in the doorway observing him with curiosity.

"I'll be working in the clinic most of the day to examine the children. I locked up until they come.

Sister Elena said it might be an hour or so. Twins are napping. Sister Elena said you were leaving, so don't hurry back on my account. And thanks for the tour."

Axel reread the first sentence of the new file that his buddy sent. Your friend is involved with the Russian mob. She is trouble.

CHAPTER 6

Axel stood as he slipped his phone in his jean pocket. The woman was a menace in spite of owning the image of a fragile angel who had somehow tarnished her halo. He remembered the bruises and wanted to ask about them, but maybe he should wait. And maybe the information wasn't the whole picture. And maybe he was making excuses for her for some unknown reason. Too many maybes for his logical brain. He'd learned a long time ago, thanks to Hollywood, that things are not always what they seem.

"Hungry?" he asked.

"Actually, I am. Just had a cup of coffee, and it was cold by the time I got to it." That smile of hers was a little more than disarming. "I showed the staff the best way to sanitize things, and they didn't appear to want or need my help. Sister said it would be another hour or so before she sent anyone to me. Wanted to wait until the twins got up from their nap. They'll come first."

"I know a place on the beach that serves a mean fry

cake and the freshest fruit anywhere. Just a short walk, if you're up to it." He noticed her slight step back and she hugged her arms. A definite sign of hesitation. PTSD could creep up on you at the weirdest times. He knew that firsthand. "But if you'd rather—"

"Let me check on the twins first and make sure Sister Elena doesn't need me for a bit."

Before he could respond, she disappeared inside the house. Was it an excuse to refuse his invitation? So be it. Although he was sure the sister didn't need her help with the full staff in place, the thought occurred to him she might use the situation to stay behind. He didn't need another woman in his life right now. The last one had nearly destroyed his soul. This one had disaster written all over her. Realizing he had a tendency to gravitate toward nuclear relationships caused him to over evaluate every woman he met. Probably why he remained aloof and alone most of the time.

He leaned back against the porch pillar near the steps and focused on the traffic, what little there was, fill the narrow street. A truck stopped in the middle of the street as the driver waved to him then yelled at a nearby car for doing the same thing. The sounds of tropical birds and the press of the morning breeze against his skin helped him remember once again why he came here. Escape. Maybe that was what Meredith wanted, too. Escape from a world that was no longer recognizable to people who longed for normalcy and peace of mind.

"I'm ready," Meredith said softly as she walked up next to him. As soon as he straightened and turned to look at her, she stepped back like he'd seen her do several times. "The twins are sleeping, and the other children will finish their homework before I give them their physicals. Sister said it would be a couple of hours before she would send them to me."

Axel nodded and hurried down the steps before he noticed she hadn't followed. "I can get my motorcycle or borrow the truck if you don't want to walk."

She joined him and eyed the spaces around her. "I love it here. I'm not sure why. Guess I'm a little in awe of the culture. People seem so happy. I'm ready."

They crossed the street and found a boardwalk that led to the beach. Colorful hammocks hung between palm trees dotting the sandy beach as it opened up before them. Once on the sand, she removed her sandals and carried them in her hand then wiggled her toes in the warmth of the beach. They passed a marked-off area where people had gathered to observe the baby sea turtles escape to the beautiful waters of the Caribbean Sea. She watched with interest then cheered with the others who encouraged their escape to the sea.

"Come on. You can do it," she called. "Almost there."

When the waves ran up onto the beach to capture the small creatures, applause broke out among the tourists and locals. Axel noticed she joined in with enthusiasm and even appeared to be happy like she'd been the night before at dinner. He really had been a jerk to her. Maybe he could make it up to her. Whatever her story might be, his probably wasn't much different. After all, he was no saint.

"This was amazing." She released a soft laugh as she followed him. "Thank you for bringing me here."

He only nodded, seeing her attention kept turning back to the waves lapping forward, almost begging for her to step into the warm waters. Taking a detour, he moved to the edge of the water, and she quickly followed, letting her feet get buried in the wet sand as brown pelicans winged their way overhead. While she was staring up at the birds, a wave rushed in and nearly knocked her down.

"Look out." He grabbed her hand and pulled her back, but the wave still managed to soak both of them from the waist down. When she burst into laughter instead of fretting about her appearance, he joined in, too. "Never turn your back on the ocean, Meredith. It has a wicked sense of humor."

"I will make a mental note of that," she said, shaking her hands free of water. "Do I need to change for the restaurant?"

"Nope. We'll eat outside, anyway, and this happens all the time. It's already hot, so you should be fine."

"Good because I'm starved."

He reached for her hand but thought better of it when her eyes widened when she seemed to focus on his hand. At the last second, he pointed to their nearby destination and walked away from her, giving her space to feel comfortable. This time, she hadn't backed away. Progress.

The owner of the beachfront restaurant had a full house but had saved one table with a view for him, just like always. Being a regular had its advantages. Coffee was brought without asking and served with some buttered cinnamon bread.

"Can I order for you, Meredith?"

"As long as it doesn't involve octopus or eel."

"The usual, Juan." The owner stole a glance at Meredith and grinned at Axel. "Oh. This is Meredith

Marshall. She's helping Sister Elena for a few days with medical exams for the children."

"That is very nice. My little girl has been fussy and running a fever lately. Are you a doctor? The doctors don't always like to come here. Can't make much money unless it is a tourist with a fat wallet."

"Nurse practitioner," she offered. "I'm not sure I can practice that kind of medicine here without a local license. But I would be happy to come check her out, Juan, after I finish at the orphanage. Or, why don't you just bring her to the clinic. I'm thinking I'll be there all day."

Juan crossed himself and kissed the crucifix hanging around his neck. "Thank you. Thank you. I will call my wife to bring her in." He hurried off to get their food and call home.

"Better be careful. You might find yourself with a line around the corner with that kind of promise. He's probably in there calling all his neighbors," Axel said as he cocked his head. "So, how does a person like you end up down here in the middle of nowhere with a nun who most likely bribed you with something? She's been known to pull those stunts from time to time. Always says God will forgive her because it's for the children."

Axel was well aware why she was here. The file his buddy sent was pretty clear she was on the run from something or someone. Was it the Russian mob? The ex-husband? Theft? Threat of more violence?

"Just a do-gooder as you so forcefully said last night. Guess the brochures and one too many romance novels convinced me I could do better than work in a big-city hospital where the almighty dollar reigns supreme."

"I'd like to apologize for my rude behavior last

night. There was no cause for that. I'm just a little protective and suspicious of strangers who show up without warning." He tried to sound easygoing, but she must have sensed something else. Pulling her hands off the table and placing them in her lap, she leaned farther back in her chair, hinting she was getting uncomfortable again.

"Apology accepted. What's your story?" She took a drink of her coffee then held the cup with both hands, as if letting the heat seep through her fingers.

The sun had begun drying her clothes, but the breeze made Axel's wet pants cold. He didn't want to complain since the bonus was sitting here in the sun with an intriguing woman.

"Went to Afghanistan with the army. Returned home. Got restless. Moved to California. That didn't work out, so I came down here on a whim and never went back."

"Family?"

"Parents are still in Missouri. Got a sister in Florida and a brother in Oklahoma. They come down here each year for a little family reunion. I try to get back for Christmas. My mom kinda insists on that. She says if I'm going to be a beach bum the rest of my life, I'd better come home at least for her favorite holiday. Going to try and get them here for Christmas this year. We'll see." He noticed how intently she listened. "What about you?"

"My parents died of cancer when I was very young. My great-aunt raised me so I have an old soul." She chuckled. "She passed away last year. Besides a few lifelong friends, in a little town called Arcadia Valley, there wasn't anyone else. We used to say it wasn't at the end of the world, but you could see it from where we lived." She cocked her head at Axel. "I envy big families. I dreamed about having sisters and brothers. Always wanted a big family, a giant Christmas tree with lots of presents, and a house full of relatives talking all at once. My favorite rerun was The Waltons."

"So, what happened?"

"Married too young. Never dated much, so first guy who came along and paid me some attention, I up and married. Didn't work out. And he really wasn't the Waltons' kind of person. He became a big-time lawyer and, you know—I just didn't fit the fast track or have the trophy wife appeal, I guess."

"He give you those bruises on your back?" He hadn't meant to ask that so bluntly or soon, but he already didn't like the guy. She paled at the question. "I saw them when you turned around as you were getting ready to come to the orphanage this morning." Lifting his chin, he stared down his nose at her. "It's none of my business, but is that what you're running away from? Is that why each time I step closer, you flinch?"

Meredith turned her eyes away and studied the waves rolling to shore. A few people were already in the water or strolling along the beach. He waited for her to respond. Maybe she wouldn't, and he guessed that would be okay, too. Finally, she nodded and turned her gaze back to him.

"Yes," she whispered. "And other things. But you were right. I can't stay long. I will make sure the children are well and the others have a decent checkup, but I did a lot to hide myself as to where I was. When the pharmacy called to check on me… I'm afraid it will be traced. I-I can't let the children see anything that might scare them further in their tough little lives. And I can't go back right now. I'm afraid of what he would do to me."

A waitress set their breakfast down carefully, mentioning to be careful, that the plates were hot then promised to be back with more coffee.

"I would have been more hospitable had I known, Meredith." He noticed she stared at a couple sitting several tables over. The man was much older than the sweet young thing sitting with him. They nodded toward Meredith, and she lifted a hand in recognition. "Friends of yours?"

"No. They were on the plane. I think maybe newlyweds? Sister Elena and I thought it an odd combination. I think they're at my hotel, too. Kind of surprised they didn't find a resort. They look like they're used to having all the amenities a resort would offer."

Axel thought the same thing, especially since they appeared to speak out of the side of their mouths to each other and casually glance their way too often. If they were lovers or newlyweds, they sure were avoiding too much touching. Even though she was a looker, there were a lot of hard angles to her, like she might be used to working out. And the man, in spite of being in his mid-to-late forties, was all muscle as well.

Maybe he'd search their room. Wouldn't be that hard to do a little recon. Nothing like keeping his skills polished in case they were more than a May-December romance.

"What do you think of the fry cakes?" he asked, shifting his attention back to Meredith.

Her mouth was full, and she nodded then waved her fork in satisfaction.

~ ~ ~ ~

"They're just eating, Gavin. Stop staring at them. The woman will get suspicious. Who is that creepy guy with her?"

"How should I know? He brought her home last night when we couldn't find her. The clerk said she left with him again this morning at sunrise. Maybe she found a lover. Wonder how that will go over back home?"

She reached across the table and pretended to stroke his hand. "If he's her lover, I'd say someone has a taste for roughness. I don't like his looks. Probably a beach bum who preys on lonely women in search of adventure."

"Maybe. He reminds me of someone though. Not sure who."

She pushed her hair away from her face as the waiter took their order then turned her attention toward the ocean. "I don't like this."

"Neither do I. Relax. This will be a walk in the park." He glanced back at the woman from the plane.

"That guy doesn't look like he knows what a walk in the park means. He could be trouble."

"Nothing we can't handle."

CHAPTER 7

The side streets were now lined with carts of fresh fruits and vegetables, along with vendors sporting clothing and accessories. A few tempted Meredith with their straw hats, handmade bead jewelry, and scarf headbands. It was all so beautiful. The smells, voices, music from a second-story window, and colorfully clad women made her feel as if she'd found Nirvana.

She jumped out of the way from a scooter driven by a girl who was no more than fourteen. For a second, there was the press of Axel's hand on her elbow as he guided her across the traffic on the narrow street where she made a mental note on how to return. A few twists and turns followed, but soon she spotted the orphanage and the lopsided sign out front, St. Francis Children's Home.

Running up the steps, she turned to notice Axel with one foot on the bottom one, staring at her through his mirrored sunglasses. His long blond hair had been partially pulled back, and his beard had several days' growth. The tan skin and toned body were exposed. With his rolled-up sleeves and open shirt that fit snugly over a tank top, she remembered that his rough touch was that of a man who used his hands to make a living.

"I'll see you later. Got some things to do. Need anything else, just have Luis text me."

"Okay," was all she could say.

He was keeping his distance and, for that, she was appreciative. Men like Axel usually had things to hide and a past that made them dangerous. At least, that's what his solemn expression hinted at, along with his constantly scanning the surroundings. Maybe she saw that in a movie. Although polite, he didn't mince words about what he thought of her last night.

He nodded and strolled away like it was no big deal living in paradise. Everyone seemed to know him from the way they waved, yelled his name, or gave him a thumbs-up. She watched him until he turned a corner toward the beach and, for the first time, wondered where he lived.

The day continued with giving the children basic checkups, considering she didn't have much to work with. Sister Elena insisted she use the clinic and whatever equipment or supplies were available. There wasn't much, but she had a feeling a little went a long way here. She remembered the restaurant owner from breakfast and pulled out the slip of paper where he'd written down his address and phone number. The mother ended up bringing the child since they lived a few blocks away. Several friends of the concerned mother also had some issues with their children and had tagged along.

It was past six by the time she met up with Sister Elena, who was setting the table for dinner. Meredith made a tray for the twins, still keeping them separated from the others until tomorrow. When she entered, carrying the tray of delicious food, they slid off the bed and ran to her, hugging her around the legs and staring up with longing with those deep-brown eyes.

"Okay. Okay. Let's have a picnic." She smiled and pointed to the floor, balancing the tray. "We'll eat on the floor and pretend it is the beach. I'll put ocean sounds on my phone."

They clapped with joy and flopped down on the floor as she awkwardly joined them. Searching for ocean waves on the phone proved easy enough, and soon they were pretending they were watching the pelicans flying overhead. They loved the game and made up things they saw on their imaginary beach.

Sister Elena joined them after baths and story time with the help of Luis and his sister. Meredith planned to spend the night so Luis peeked in to say good night. This tipped off the twins it was time for bed. Pedro jumped to his feet and hugged Meredith's legs until she lifted him with one arm. Rosa repeated the motion, but instead of lifting her, she reluctantly pointed to the bed. The sad eyes and trembling lips changed Meredith's mind. With some degree of difficulty, she managed to lift her into the other arm.

"You children are too heavy." Sister Elena tried to take Pedro, but his grip tightened around Meredith's neck.

Meredith faked choking as she awkwardly flopped on the bed, causing a burst of laughter to escape from the twins. "The other children are already in bed," she explained. "And you two are so much better," she said after landing kisses on their heads. "I'm happy."

"Tell Sister Elena we need to stay in here one more night so we can be together," Rosa whispered in her ear as she wrinkled her nose then nodded her head.

Pedro leaned in to whisper in her ear as well. "Please. Please. Please."

"Sister Elena, although the fever appears to be gone, I think one more night isolated from the others would be a good idea." The twins had no idea she'd already decided it was her plan all along.

"I hoped they could go back. I'm too tired to stay in here with them, Meredith. I have only one helper tonight who will watch the children upstairs."

"Can I stay with them? I'm spending the night anyway. That way if someone else comes down with the crud, then you won't have to send for me."

Sister Elena put her hands on her hips and clicked her tongue in disapproval. "What have you rascals been telling Ms. Meredith?"

"Just that we still feel a little sick," Rosa said, holding up her forefinger and thumb to show how little.

"Well…"

"Thank you, Sister," they said in unison, causing the nun to try and suppress a grin by clamping her mouth into a straight line.

"Meredith, you have been here all day. You must be exhausted. Wouldn't you like to go back to the hotel for shower and clean clothes?"

"I'll go in the morning. I'm fine. Not sure I could make it there before falling asleep."

"Very well, then. Sweet dreams. And you two are back in your room tomorrow night."

Their head bobs of acceptance indicated they would go.

Once Sister Elena left, the twins yawned then begged for a story.

~ ~ ~ ~

Axel let himself in through the French doors of the May-December couple. Picking the lock was not a problem. Fortunately, they were on the first floor, and the tropical garden covered his approach and entry to their room. He had followed them around most of the day.

Several hours on the beach convinced him they were not married or romantically involved. With the skimpy bathing suit the woman wore and her curvy body, no man would be able to resist applying sunscreen to that delicate skin. Although he glanced her way from time to time and leaned in to talk, she appeared to ignore him and read her magazine. They never touched indicating attraction. And as far as her attention to him, he wasn't a bad-looking guy: fit, slim, and very tan. He occasionally swam and came back, only to be handed a towel by the fake Mrs.

Shopping took up the afternoon, with her buying a few things. She didn't strike him as a trophy wife of a rich guy—otherwise she'd be buying out the place. They strolled by the orphanage several times, stopping to study a map, which, in itself, was suspicious. Who did that anymore? A brochure showing various sites to take in while they were in Belize would have been a much better cover. After pretending to glance around as if lost, they soon moved on. Later, they ate at a little café down the road from the orphanage.

Although the orphanage was practically in town, it

wasn't a place where tourists usually trekked. The area consisted of mostly residential homes with mom-and-pop stores. To him, it was the best of their little slice of heaven in Belize. No fast-food restaurants. No expensive souvenir stores with T-shirts made in China. No expensive side trips into the rain forest with "real" Mayan guides to give you the trip of a lifetime. Here, everything remained authentic. Those two were not.

He didn't worry about them walking in on him. The couple had reservations at the one fancy eatery by the ocean. It was expensive, and your experience usually lasted several hours besides the wait, no matter if you had a reservation. He waited until they left, the woman dressed in a strapless dress that must have cost a bundle, and the fake husband sporting dress khakis and a white shirt, open at the collar. It made his tan appear darker.

They never unpacked. Each put their dirty clothes in a separate plastic bag. A couple would have shoved them in the same bag to wash later. The bathroom also was too neat, as if they were respecting each other's space. He was keenly aware that this room had two queen beds instead of one king. Odd for newlyweds. Both appeared to have been used. He pulled out the drawer in the nightstand and lifted out a condom.

"There's always hope, huh, buddy?" he mumbled. Next, he ran his hand under the top of the drawer and felt something cold and hard. Pulling it free of the Velcro, he retrieved a Walther P99. "Heck of a thing to take on your honeymoon."

He searched the woman's luggage and there didn't appear to be any lacy undergarments. In fact, the sleeping attire appeared to be pj's with cat designs.

Again. Not very romantic for a honeymoon.

The room was just too neat. Even the small fridge still had the hotel snacks, booze, and soft drinks. There was a receipt for breakfast, so why would they show up on the beach to order at the same place he took Meredith? No passports that he found. Might be in the hotel safe, but such things were off-limits, and asking the staff, although they were usually cooperative, might get him into trouble with the local police. He certainly didn't need any extra attention.

He secured a glass and a coffee cup edged with lipstick. Once he got back to his place, he'd lift their prints and send them to his buddy to see if they were in the system. As he backed out of the garden French doors, he double-checked he hadn't left evidence of his visit. Everything was just as he found it. This was his specialty. Making his way back to his boat, he quickly lifted the prints, photographed them, and sent them off. Hopefully, he'd hear back soon. In the meantime, he needed to get these back and place them precisely where he found them. That would be the tricky part.

Several hours later, he showed up at the orphanage. The doors were still unlocked, which was odd this time of night. Then a voice from the dark side of the porch caused him to pivot as he prepared himself for an attack.

"It's just me, Axel." Sister Elena said.

"You know better than sneak up on me like that. I could have hurt you," he growled as he walked over to the sister and helped her wiggle out of the swing.

"Nonsense. You are a good man. Now, walk me to my room. I am tired and worried."

He escorted her as far as her door and spotted a dim

light in the spare bedroom where the twins had been earlier in the day. "Are the twins still downstairs?"

She nodded and patted his arm. "Yes. Meredith is with them, and Luis's sister is upstairs. I don't know what we would have done without her today. Do you know what your friend at the restaurant did?"

Axel could feel his forehead wrinkle in bad news.

Sister Elena went on, "Apparently, he got the word out that our clinic was open. Meredith worked all day. She has appointments scheduled until the end of the week. I think the people like her." She grinned and hugged her arms in delight. "She came back after dinner, exhausted. Go. Check on her. She may need something. Be kind."

"I always am."

"Not so much to her. I'm going to bed. Lock up on your way out." She patted his cheek.

He bent down to kiss her lightly. "Why are you worried?" He looked her square in her tiny eyes.

"This place. I didn't get much support on my trip to the States. Things are tough everywhere. We need more donations."

"I'll be getting a check soon, Sister. I'll be able to help more. You can have all of it, if you want it."

"You've already done so much. God will provide. I need to trust He'll send us a miracle."

"Not sure that will happen," he decided offhandedly.

"Don't forget, we're taking the children to the Turtle Festival on Friday night. It wouldn't hurt you to clean up and be a little more presentable." She pointed to the spare bedroom. "Maybe she can give you back a little faith in people."

He rolled his eyes. "I have you. I don't need anyone

else messing up my life."

"Ha!" she snapped then disappeared into her room.

Standing for a good minute until he heard the good sister saying her prayers, he moved toward the spare bedroom. He wasn't prepared for what he saw.

CHAPTER 8

The spare room was bathed in a night-light near the open door. The single bed where the twins had slept earlier was empty. Alarmed, he stepped closer then spotted Meredith, lying on the floor with the twins, clinging to each other as they faced their new protector. Her arm lay across them; Rosa had snuggled under her chin. The overhead fan, shaped like palm branches, turned with a soft clicking sound. An open window let in a cool breeze. A sheet had been pulled over the twins, but Meredith's arm and body lay exposed.

Wondering if she were cold, he pulled a small lap cover off the bed and spread it over her. She exhaled and partially rolled over then her eyes opened. With a gasp, she grabbed protectively at the twins.

"It's me, Meredith. I'm sorry I startled you." He moved to the other side of the twins and squatted next to them then felt their heads. "Cool as a cucumber." He loved it when he could see them sleeping, which wasn't often.

He had rocked them to sleep in the past, but those times were few and far between, since they were getting older. Running his hand across Pedro's dark hair, he noticed Meredith staring at him. In the dappled light touching parts of her face, he was reminded of the pictures in the chapel of Madonna and Child. This woman was no Madonna. "Aren't you uncomfortable?"

She lay back down and tucked her arm under her head and pierced his common sense with those soft eyes. Careful.

"Yes," she whispered as she turned toward the little boy and girl in her care. "But they wanted to be together one more night and for me to join them. We had a picnic on the floor earlier, with ocean waves and everything." A soft chuckle escaped her lips. "I fell asleep while they were still talking to each other. It sounded like music to me. Sweet. Melodic. Innocent of all wrong." She lifted her eyes back to him. "I didn't have time to make arrangements to move on today or talk to Sister Elena about not wanting the job. Before I knew it, I'd agreed to see a few more people the next few days. I won't mention our earlier conversation to her."

"About that. I was out of line. I was being judgmental, and the sister doesn't allow that. Stay a few more days and get a feel for the place. It could be more work than you expected, though, and, to be honest, the pay sucks." The little boy rolled toward him and opened his eyes slightly. "Go back to sleep, little guy."

"Rock me," he moaned softly. "Please." Axel stood and lifted the small child into his arms then walked over to the rocking chair in the corner. The squeak of the chair woke Rosa, and she immediately felt for her brother. She called out to him, and her twin straightened up in Axel's arms. In seconds, she was on her feet.

Meredith pushed herself up with some difficulty and then scooped the child into her arms. Fortunately, this room had been a nursery and had a second rocking chair. "Come on. Your brother is right here with Axel. See?" She nearly fell into the chair which wobbled, but Axel reached out and placed his hand on the armrest. "Thank you. See there? Your brother has captured Axel."

"And I have captured you," she said, snuggling closer as Meredith wrapped her arms around her.

She sang softly as the child closed her eyes. Axel couldn't help but scrutinize her intently, wondering if the information he'd received was all wrong, maybe misconstrued by his buddy, Jake. Had he judged a book by its cover? Could she be for real or just playing a part to escape the Russian mob? Whatever part she was playing, the woman was damn good at it. Even he was falling for it—or was it for her? Her soft singing relaxed him until he realized Pedro had returned to sleep and Rosa as well. The words now came intermittently, as Meredith's breathing deepened into her own kind of sleep.

Axel memorized the curve of her jawline, the wavy hair falling down around her shoulders, and her slender arms cradling the child. But the temptation to sleep was too great after hearing her sing and the warmth of Pedro in his arms. Leaning his head back, he decided to rest for just a little while then would move the children to the bed so Meredith could rest. But when he awoke, sunlight filled the room, and the twins were staring at him in childlike curiosity. Each took a hand and pulled him to his feet. He stretched and noticed the empty rocker next to him.

"Where's Miss Meredith?" He yawned.

"Gone," they said and they ran from the room.

Gone? Had she actually taken his advice and left? That it mattered to him put him on edge.

"Where's Meredith?" he asked Sister Elena who was clearing the table.

She twisted her mouth in irritation, lifting plates in each hand. "She left several hours ago. What did you say to her last night? If you have hurt her feelings, I will—"

"Calm down. I didn't do a thing. I even apologized like you told me to."

"Apologize? I said be nice. What did you need to apologize for?" She set the dishes back on the table and planted her hands on her hips. Often, when she did this, he imagined a rooster ready to flog an intruder. Nothing to take lightly.

"It doesn't matter. Did she say where she was going?"

"It does matter because I need her here. You need her here. What about your dreams and plans for the future? You can't do it alone. This place needs a full-time staff. A staff I can't afford."

"And how do you think you're going to afford her?"

"God will provide," she stormed, pointing to the ceiling.

"You keep saying that and I can barely keep the place patched together."

"We need a miracle."

"We need money. I wish I had more, Sister, but I

don't," he snapped. That seemed to calm her down.

"I know." She opened her arms and motioned for him to come to her. "You are a guardian angel, Axel. I say thanks for you each night and pray for your happiness."

He refused to be hugged like one of her children and shook his head then raised his stubborn chin. "Did you tell her you couldn't pay her? You can't expect her to work here for free."

She shook her finger at him. "A miracle. That's all."

He threw his hands in the air and grunted. "Did Luis take her back to the hotel?"

"No. He was cooking breakfast. She took one of those tricycle taxis. She'll be back later. I told her to explore our little town, relax, enjoy the beach before she comes to work."

"Work," he barked. "Here?"

"The clinic, of course. She has appointments. I thought it would be okay. She isn't charging anything for her services so it shouldn't be a problem. I'll work on getting her a license. The mayor owes me a favor and the governor-general owes the mayor a favor. See? I told you it would work out." He headed out through the big living room as she called to him. "Don't forget the festival this weekend. Meredith and I will need help with the children. Wouldn't hurt for you to help her today," she called after him.

Ignoring her was nearly impossible so he picked up speed and barreled through the front doors. "Women," he fumed as he located his motorcycle and eased out into the morning traffic.

All he wanted to do was go to his boat, get cleaned up, and find some breakfast—alone. But his computer was waiting for him to connect with his friend stateside.

"You look like hell, my friend. What have you been doing?" His voice sounded amused. "Is Sister Elena working you overtime for free, or are you chasing that pretty nurse that has you compiling a dossier on her?"

"Always the jokes. What have you got for me?" He pulled out a wooden stool and sat in front of the computer. "Were you able to get a read on the fingerprints?"

"Yes and no. I did get into the data bank and even called in some favors. However, it was locked up tight, and I was told they didn't exist. Nothing to report, in a nutshell. Maybe, if you could get a picture of them, I might be able to run down another rabbit hole, so to speak."

"They are registered as Mr. and Mrs. Flynn. I'm guessing that is fake, too." Axel had told him the night before how he came by the fingerprints.

"Most likely. There's something else you need to know. You're not going to like it."

"Meredith's husband…"

"Ex-husband. Divorced."

"There's a missing person's alert for her. The ex is under suspicion of being involved. She has several girlfriends who have pushed the police to investigate. They're organizing searches. She's all over the news. Not only that, this afternoon, her car was found under a dry-creek bridge. Her purse, wallet, and phone were there. To top it off, there was blood in there, too. It won't take long to trace that, along with viable DNA samples."

"A setup?"

"That's my guess. This woman wanted to disappear

big-time."

"What about the Russians?"

"The husband thinks they've killed her because he owed them money. The amount was 100K. Took him a few days to confess that. Now, he's probably a marked man, too."

Axel whistled. "That's a lot of money."

"He mortgaged the house before they split up then lost that plus the car because he gambled. Rumor has it, your girl is up to her eyeballs with those guys. To make things even more interesting, your Florence Nightingale came into some money just before the divorce."

"She has no family. Where would she get money?"

"You're right. No savings, thanks to the ex. I'm guessing she did the Russians a favor. One thing the hubby didn't get his hands on was some money her great-aunt left her. Came to about two hundred grand. Because it was inheritance, the judge ruled in her favor and said he couldn't have one dime. It's gone, too."

"Let me guess. Paid them to get her out: new papers, passport, the works. They gave her a new life, maybe she paid off the ex's debt as well and hightailed it out of Dodge."

"Yep. My thoughts exactly since I didn't find any trace of extra money. The thing is, if that DNA and blood comes back like I think it will, the guy will be charged with murder and sent away for a long time. There are Russians on the inside, and you know what will happen to him there. Think she knew about the setup they were creating?"

"Hard to say." Axel stewed about the new information. "Russians don't like to be crossed. She doesn't strike me as the type to take revenge. Also doesn't live the lifestyle. Here on a budget, I think. Not a big spender so far. Maybe set enough money aside to get out when the time is right. She thinks I'm poor—"

This drew a deep laugh from his friend. "If she only knew. Anyway, my sources say the feds have gone to several banks searching for something. No luck there. I'm thinking they are trying to find evidence against the ex. Maybe a hidden account. If he's got one of those, either the Russians will soon have it, or he'll be finding himself at the bottom of a lake someplace with an anchor around his neck—and the Russians will have that money, too."

"Who do you think this fake couple are?"

"Don't have enough intel to determine what the scenario might be. Maybe they're after you. Ever think of that?"

"I'm always thinking of that. Thanks. Call if you find out anything else."

CHAPTER 9

Letting the water roll across her sore muscles did a lot for a foggy brain. Meredith stood under the hot spray long enough that the water turned from hot to warm. She quickly washed her hair then wrapped a towel around her head and a terry cloth robe around her damp body. It had been a splurge to buy it. The coffee was ready in the little coffeemaker on the bathroom counter. Even with creamer and two packs of sugar, it tasted like crude oil. She ended up pouring it into the sink. Now she wished she'd taken Luis up on eating breakfast before she'd left the orphanage.

Rosa had been the first to stir awake. After a few kisses and snuggles, Meredith had set her down and noticed Pedro waking up. Axel slept so peacefully holding the child in his arms that she could only admire at how ruggedly handsome he was. The notion occurred to her that those same arms probably had a love interest waiting for him somewhere. Part of her hoped it wasn't true, just in case—she didn't want to think about that kind of future since it would be impossible for her. Her

73

choices in love had been a disaster. Her auntie had warned her about Nathan, but she'd married him anyway. It didn't take long to realize what a mistake she'd made, but she kept trying.

Pedro reached for her, and she lifted him into her arms. He laid his head onto her shoulder, stretching his hand down to touch Rosa, who patted his leg. She couldn't get over how cute they were or how much love they held for each other. The questions formed once again what it would take to adopt them. Deep down, she knew being a person on the run, without a home or country, posed a great deal of obstacles. Someone much better than her must be available for these precious babies.

The man sound asleep before her cared for these children. It was obvious how much all of them adored him. Even when he was gruff, a slight grin toyed with the corner of his mouth. She didn't want to think about his physical attributes, either.

Today would be another busy one at the clinic. Yesterday had been fulfilling and exhausting. The activity and nonstop work had soothed her turbulent soul. In spite of sleeping on the floor and in a rocking chair, she'd rested for the first time in a couple of months. Remembering the restaurant on the beach convinced her to make it her first stop. Drinking good coffee and watching the waves crash ashore would be the recharge she needed. Maybe she could even stop at the little boutique near the orphanage to get the dress she'd seen in the window the day before.

She had a few hours before she needed to open the clinic, so she finished pulling on her shorts and tropical-inspired blouse. Her wet hair needed a quick brushing.

The breezes would dry it soon enough and keep her cool in the meantime. When she stepped out onto the sidewalk in front of the hotel, she came to terms with how happy she was here. In spite of Axel wanting her to leave, maybe it would be possible to right all her wrongs and stay. What might she do to prove herself worthy to him? And why had that become important to her?

With sandals in hand, she strolled across the beach, listening to a mix of crashing ocean waves, screeching seagulls, and pelicans. The beach was nearly empty, and the sway of palm trees pulled her closer to get her feet wet. The warm sand pushed between her toes as the wave foam splashed on her legs. She continued along the edge until the restaurant came into view. As she moved farther up onto the beach, something caught her eye.

A man rose out of the water, pushing his hair back from his face before moving forward in spite of the waves trying to pull him back. His body glistened in the morning light and, for the first time, Meredith could admire Axel's strong and fit body without embarrassment. This was a man who worked hard for a living. The self-confident push through the determined waves and his eyes squinting against the sunlight gave Meredith a moment's pause.

As he came closer to the beach, his legs became visible. Not only were they muscled, but tattoos trailed around on his thigh. The design resembled Celtic emblems she'd seen over the years. She also noticed, for the first-time, a Celtic cross hanging around his neck. Could Sister Elena have insisted he wear it since he worked for her? He didn't strike her as a religious man or someone who could be forced to do anything he didn't want. But it was also true the woman had him wrapped around her finger and most likely used the children to maintain control.

The decision to keep her presence invisible evaporated when he spotted her and waved after toweling himself off. She wasn't sure why such a simple act gave her the shivers and heatstroke at the same time. This tropical place must be having an adverse effect on her ability to think straight. He placed the beach towel around his waist like a sarong and moved toward her, wringing his blond hair free of water.

"Morning." His eyes narrowed at her. His gaze traveled slowly from her bare feet up her legs and continued to her face, as if he were deciding if she was worth the trouble.

She felt exposed, nervous, and guilty. "I'm on my way to breakfast." She turned her attention away from him since his half-naked body made her uncomfortable. "Thought I'd try breakfast at your place again. The coffee in my room was not the best. Care to join me?"

"Sure. Your treat, I hope." He grinned mischievously and pulled on the tank top he grabbed off the beach towel a second earlier. "Didn't bring my wallet."

"Of course. I wanted to return the favor anyway." They moved toward the outdoor restaurant, and Meredith spotted the newlyweds strolling down the beach. When she waved to them, they casually returned the gesture then linked hands. "I would have thought they would sleep in or something," she said sarcastically.

"Something being the key word," he added then chuckled.

Heat traveled up her throat and face. "Oh. I meant…"

He continued to grin at her, eyebrows lifting.

"Guess I did mean a more meaningful something." She let a light laugh escape, too, releasing her nervousness.

The owner of the restaurant rushed to seat them. "Anything you want is on the house, Miss Marshall. Thank you so much for helping my little one. She is much better today. I'm glad it wasn't serious. My wife said she tried to pay you, but you would take nothing."

"I'm not licensed here, Juan. I'm only helping Sister Elena for a few days. I'll be leaving soon."

"We will win you over. It has gotten out you might be staying for good. Sister Elena has told everyone." Juan beamed. "We need you here. I will make a space for you right here with this beach bum every day if you like. He is a lone wolf who needs some manners and a gentle lady."

"Let's not get ahead of ourselves, Juan," Axel instructed. "Bring us some coffee, or I'll stop fishing for you each week."

Juan winked at Meredith then hurried off.

"No girlfriend or wife, then?" Please say no.

"Not at the moment, and never been married, nor do I want to be. How about you? Think you'll bite the bullet again someday?"

"Not sure I can afford another screwup. I think maybe I need some time to decide what I want and see where that leads me." She looked out at the ocean waves and the swaying palm trees. "Do you ever get used to this?"

It was obvious how smitten she'd become with this place. Her faraway gaze toward the horizon reflected being more at peace than when she first arrived. It led Axel to wonder what had happened in the last few months to make her this cautious and afraid. Granted, someone had used her as a punching bag one too many times, and she was most likely broke. There remained another element he needed to know. Did Meredith Marshall pose a danger to those he loved at the orphanage? Even though she had gotten under his skin, that wouldn't be enough to save her if she brought disaster or pain to his eclectic family.

With the coffee poured and plates of eggs and fruit set before them, their conversation slowed. But curiosity got the best of him, and he steered the conversation toward interrogation. "Why here? Sister Elena said when she saw where you worked, you didn't plan on leaving. What changed your mind?"

She chewed her food slower, as if she might be thinking of a reason.

"My ex was harassing me. Even though we got a divorce, he still wanted a relationship: physical and financial."

He noticed she began to stir her food with her fork before shifting her attention toward the ocean. "I was afraid he'd talk me into something I didn't want to do. My heart had been broken long before we divorced. I was in debt because of my schooling, his gambling habit and my credit tanked. He got into some trouble and expected me to bail him out—like always."

Axel had reached across the table and laid a hand on

hers when he saw a tear pool in the corner of her eye. "Is that when he hit you?"

She turned her focus to his hand on hers and, for a moment, he expected her to pull away, but she didn't. "Axel, I know you mean well, but I can't talk about this. I did some things I shouldn't have, to get away. I love it here and want to stay, but I'm afraid if I do, there will be trouble. I've screwed up my life until now, and this is heaven. If I can last a little longer, I will be free from this nightmare."

"If you're afraid your ex will come here, I can help you."

"No one can help me, Axel. I've got to do this on my own. Maybe then I can help Sister Elena."

Axel decided to drop it and enjoy the morning as he removed his hand from hers. When he'd spotted her on the beach, she'd reminded him of a beautiful soul, lost in paradise. The wind toying with her auburn hair had turned it wild and curly, but she didn't bother to tame it. Although there was nothing fancy about her, she exuded a kind of beauty Mother Nature gives only a few people. Even now, as she spoke, he wanted to study her, enjoy how her mouth moved when she spoke, listen to the tone of her voice, and drink in the way she turned those hazel-green eyes toward the ocean as if searching for magic. Why did he feel as if he didn't want to believe any of the information his friend had given him?

"I'd better go," she said, checking her watch. "I wanted to stop at a little shop I spotted yesterday before I open the clinic. Sister Elena said something about taking the children to the Turtle Festival on Friday and could use my help. I probably should get a dress. I mostly brought casual stuff that's pretty worn. Thought I'd treat myself to one souvenir. Will you be there?"

"Highlight of my week. I don't have a choice. The good sister has a way of enlisting help, even if you'd rather stay home and read a book."

"Ah. A reader. A man after my own heart." When he couldn't help but narrow his eyes in amusement, she blushed. "I mean. Oh, that didn't come out right. I just meant—"

"I know what you meant. Do me a favor, Ms. Meredith Marshall."

She nodded and waited patiently.

"Don't be giving that heart of yours to anyone too soon. I might like a crack at it when you're ready." He stood and stared down at her. "I got a few things to do this week before the festival. Thanks for breakfast."

This time, she smiled broadly at him but said nothing. Why on earth had he said such a thing? He didn't need another woman trying to change him or sucking the life out of him. Avoiding those kinds of relationships for the last eighteen months had made him a better man. Then he went and said something he had no intention of following through on. Meredith, vulnerable and pretty, gave him an irresistible urge to flirt. He decided to get such nonsense into check before he made a risky situation worse. Trouble was his middle name, and he didn't want any more of it right now.

CHAPTER 10

Slipping in through the side door of the clinic, she spotted several people waiting out front. Little faces pressed against the glass. Her heart warmed at their expectation to come inside. But first she went into the small office to inspect the red-flowered dress she'd found for the festival.

Trying it on in the dressing room had drawn compliments from the small woman who owned the shop. The hem hit the middle of her calf, and the owner showed her how to wear the sleeves down on her arms, exposing her shoulders. It wasn't as expensive as she'd feared, and she agreed to the price. The clerk showed her a matching necklace and earrings created from seashells. They were beautiful and, if at home, she'd have bought them in an instant. But those days were gone and, for the time being, she needed to be careful of every penny. Maybe, if things worked out, it could be a reward for her endurance of a difficult situation. Besides, the dress was pretty enough to stand alone. She had a pair of dress sandals that would be perfect. The children wouldn't care.

But, what about Axel? Would he notice? And why did she even care? He was a flash in the pan. Remembering those kinds of facts would go a long way to reaching her goal of independence without the help of a man. For a moment, at breakfast, she'd caved and fallen for those blue eyes and rugged good looks. She got the impression from the way Sister Elena manipulated him that he had his own checkered past. Even so, it would be nice if he was impressed. Just once, she'd enjoy being the one who could overwhelm a man instead of the other way around.

When the side door clicked open, Meredith peeked to see the sister come in using her cane. Before she could shove the dress back in the bag, the older woman entered and fingered the dress.

"You will be stunning in this. Will you wear it to the festival?"

"I was planning on it. Most of the things I brought aren't very festive. Thought I'd treat myself this once."

"Thank you for all your help. Now, before you open the clinic today, I want to make you an offer."

"What kind of offer, Sister Elena?"

"An offer to stay. Work here for our people, the children of the orphanage, and even for the businesses who have tourists. It will be good."

"I do love it here, Sister. But there are things I have to get rid of in my life to stay. I'm not sure when that is going to happen. I'm afraid it would be trouble and interfere with the work needing to be done."

She shook her finger at her. "My dear Meredith, nothing is too big for God to solve. I am waiting for a miracle. I think you are it. And Axel can take care of everything else. He always does."

A warmth of gratitude and acceptance washed over her as she placed her hand over her heart. "I don't think anyone ever called me a miracle." She took the woman's free hand and squeezed. "I am not your miracle, Sister Elena."

"Yes, my child, you are, and I want you to stay. I have no money to pay you, but I will soon. My benefactors like to send money at the last minute to claim the deduction on their income taxes. Then, I can pay you. In the meantime, I can house and feed you. There's a room in the back here you can make your own if you like. You would be great company and a good influence on that rascal, Axel."

"I think Axel prefers I keep moving on." She led the sister to a chair. "He seems pretty protective of you and the children. How long has he been here?"

"Forever," she said, propping herself on the cane. "Well, except when he was in the army and then California. But he found his way back."

"Forever? What about his family in Missouri?"

"A very sad story. They traveled down here on a mission trip. A hurricane came through, and they drowned. I found Axel barely alive. His little body was broken and so was his spirit. He was only three years old. Back then, I was very young. Sister Mary Margaret was my mentor, friend. She's the one that started the orphanage."

"There used to be two of you here?"

"Yes of course. It is the way of our order. But when she died, no help came to replace her. I wanted to keep going and no one said stop, and here we are."

"So what happened to Axel after his parents died?"

She exhaled slowly as her face emptied of joy. "Just

like the twins. I nursed him back to health and, after many months, I decided he would be my child. Always rebellious," she said, waving a finger at her, "mischievous, and with the energy of three boys." She shook her head. "No one in his extended family offered to take him, so this became his home." Her eyes turned toward the ceiling. "I needed him badly. Without him, I would not have the building we now live in or this clinic. He paid for everything."

"Everything? But I thought he was just a handyman. Someone who you gave parttime work."

"Well, those things are true, but he likes to work. He has ghosts of his own, so he keeps busy. This is a good place to escape such things," she said. "But, I'm afraid even he cannot keep up with the expenses. Thankfully, all his work is free, so I can keep the staff. Even Luis doesn't get paid as often as he should and has had to take a second job to make ends meet. I was hoping we could buy the lot next door to make a garden and play area. I have many ideas to generate money, but, as you know, it takes money to make money. Even Axel has big ideas."

"I thought he was a beach bum or one of those surfer guys who follow the waves around the world." She felt stunned. "Not that there's anything wrong with those activities. I only thought—well…"

"To be honest, he has been those things, but mostly he is my knight in shining armor, and I hope he never strays too far away. I'm sure he'd like to show you one of his projects. It's quite spectacular. It's on hold since he's had to help support us. The church can no longer afford us, so I have to make do."

She experienced a mixture of confusion, irritation,

and betrayal at this new information concerning Axel. Further proof she shouldn't be trusted in the handsome men department. No telling where he got his money. Probably some kind of drug lord or black-market businessman. He certainly had that vibe, come to think of it.

The sister reached out a bony hand for assistance to stand. "He wouldn't want me to say anything, but he set up a scholarship fund for the children to go to college if they wish. I'm not sure how he manages. Bless him." She squeezed her eyes shut then opened them wide and arched a mischievous eyebrow. "I think you two are a good team."

"I think you're trying to be a matchmaker. I'm not ready for another relationship, Sister. Remember, I told you on the plane I come with baggage and not in a good way."

"God is in the details."

"Not this time. I made a mess, and I have to do this on my own. I don't want to take a chance on bringing trouble here."

"A miracle. You'll see."

Meredith walked her to the side door and offered to escort her back to the adjoining orphanage. The sister refused and insisted she take care of her patients. One more time, she insisted Meredith was the miracle she'd been waiting for.

After she made sure the sister got safely inside, Meredith continued to stare after her, knowing the secret she carried held the answers to the sister's prayers, both financially and spiritually. But would it be in time? When would it be safe to breathe? To live like a normal person again? Did she even know what a normal person was anymore?

How could she consider working for free, no home, no place to run, few funds to survive on until she got the all clear? A man she'd just met, who one minute made it clear he didn't like her then soon after began flirting with her, might be her kryptonite. Add in a nun who professed to have the ear of God and would make her stay here to fulfill her dreams. The images of the twins flashed before her. Could she leave them? Would she be a fit mother? Was it possible to fall in love with such an idea this soon?

Best to get busy and pretend this was just another day. Deep down, she knew it was more than just another day in paradise.

~ ~ ~ ~

It was a dumb thing to do and, although he knew this without a doubt, Axel did it anyway. Maybe because he was getting soft or an easy touch for a pretty face and a sad story. When he walked by the boutique after running some errands, the owner came out and gave him the receipt Meredith had left on the counter. No credit card. She paid cash. Figures. When he asked to see the dress she bought, there wasn't another one, but the owner showed him a picture in the catalog she ordered from.

"I saw her with you yesterday. Can you give her the receipt? I hear she has the clinic open. We are so happy. Now I will not have to take my grandchildren forty miles to see a doctor."

"I think it's just temporary. Do you have something to go with this dress?"

"Oh yes. I tried to get her to buy some jewelry, but I think she was short on cash. Would you like to see it?" She winked at him. "She plans to wear the dress to the festival. I think you will be impressed."

Not only did he want to see it, Axel bought the necklace and earrings. They weren't expensive but might be considered a want rather than a need if you were short on cash. At least she didn't use a credit card to give herself away to the unknown folks back home.

The rest of the week, he worked on his boat or took a few tourists out to fish or snorkel along the reef. He dropped by the orphanage only when he knew Meredith would be at the clinic. Not seeing her for a few days helped him clear his guilty conscience about spying on her personal history. It also helped him toughen up against female manipulation again, even if was unintended on her part.

He walked to the orphanage come Friday evening, carrying the gift box. Wearing his pair of good khaki pants and the turquoise shirt he'd purchased several days earlier gave him a sharper image, he decided as he saw himself in one of the store windows. His sandals were worn, but he didn't want to break in a new pair just to impress a woman who most likely was on her way out of his life. If she didn't approve, it wouldn't be the first time a woman snubbed his avant-garde style.

His opinion changed when he walked into the gathering room of the orphanage. In that moment, with her standing there in the red flowery dress, wearing a radiant expression on her face, his suspicious brain gave in to his heart that had grown hard and unforgiving for way too long. The thought occurred to him that maybe she was his miracle, not Sister Elena's.

CHAPTER 11

Even with the squeal of excitement when the children saw him and nearly knocked him over when they surrounded him, Axel could not tear his attention away from the woman before him. She'd pushed her hair back on one side with a small red flower that matched her dress. Those bare shoulders sparked a desire he hadn't felt in a long time.

"Come see Miss Meredith, Axel. We made her surprises to wear tonight." Pedro tugged at his hand.

They pushed him forward until he stood before her. Lightly applied lipstick managed to make him want to remove it with her in his arms. A vision of candlelight, the waves crashing to shore, and breezes touching their entwined bodies flashed before him and melted away just as quickly when the children raised her hand.

"We made her bracelets for tonight. Aren't they pretty?" one of the older children asked.

He took advantage of the opportunity presented to him and took her hand in his to examine the ragged twists of twine and beads. "Not bad, guys. I bet it took a lot of work," he said, turning her hand this way and that. He met her eyes and received a warm smile but never offered to pull away. "Guess what I brought her will pale in comparison." He dropped her hand and pretended to be forlorn and rejected. Shaking his head and shuffling his feet, Axel put a hand in his pocket and withdrew a box. "I thought maybe Miss Meredith would like something to go with that pretty dress."

The children covered their mouths in surprise.

Rosa patted his leg. "It's okay, Axel. She will like it even if it isn't as good as ours."

"Thank you, Rosa." He tilted his head and extended the gift to Meredith. "The owner of the store grabbed me when I walked by. You left your receipt. She recommended this."

Meredith opened the plain brown box tied with ribbon. She lifted the necklace out with one finger, causing the children to coo with delight.

"Put it on," they encouraged.

"Wait. What is this?" She pulled out the matching earrings with a combination of tiny pearls and red beads. "These are lovely, Axel. Thank you," she said, with pure delight shining in her eyes.

He relieved her of the necklace, and she pivoted to let him fasten it around her neck as she lifted her hair. It took restraint not to let his fingers linger on her slender neck and lean in to taste those smooth shoulders. Stepping away, she quickly added the earrings then shoved her hands on her hips for the approval of the children who gave loud hoops and howls of delight.

When she turned back to him, he saw something remarkable. Unlike the woman who arrived nearly a week and a half ago, who stumbled with embarrassment at the airport luggage carousel and was more than a little unsure of herself, she now wore a kind of happiness and peace missing that first day.

He took a chance and reached out to her. Without hesitation she slipped her hand in his, and he twirled her around like Cinderella at the ball, meeting her prince for the first time. When he drew her back, they connected on a new playing field. Someone cleared their throat; they dropped hands and sheepishly caught the devious smirk of Sister Elena.

"Don't you two look handsome," she said, cocking her head, lifting her thin eyebrows, and batting her eyelids in amusement. "Shall we go?"

The giggles echoed throughout the house again as honking came from the front. Sister Elena waved her cane then ushered the children toward the door. "Come. Uncle Luis has secured the shuttle from the hotel for the evening. They even filled it with gas for us." She turned her attention back to Meredith. "Our bus is in the shop more than on the road. Remind me tomorrow the children should write thank-you notes." She turned her attention to the children. "Maybe you can make some bracelets for the hotel staff, too."

They moved in quick, organized steps, along with a great deal of head bobbing at the plan for more bracelet creations. The children boarded the small shuttle bus with Luis waving them on enthusiastically. Sister Elena allowed Axel to offer his hand in assistance, but when she reached the landing, she turned toward him and held out her hand for him stop.

"Oh no. We are full. Isn't that right, Luis?" she said, poking the man with a wickedly sharp finger.

"Yes. It is true," he said with a shrug and jutted out

his bottom lip. Then he peeked around the sister and chuckled at Axel who now wore a creased brow of confusion.

"Why don't you two young people go along the beach to the festival. It isn't far." She poked Luis again. "Close the door. Time to go."

As the shuttle slowly pulled away, the children waved out the window and the singing of their driver drifted along as they disappeared down the street.

"I think Sister Elena is playing matchmaker. Sorry about that." Axel shoved his hands in his pockets to help him resist taking her hand and leading her toward the beach. But her shy expression and slightly blushed face indicated she picked up on the trick.

"She is very fond of you. Why did you lie to me earlier about your family?"

And just like that, she knocked the wind out of him. Sister Elena had been talking too much again.

"No one likes to be an orphan. I wasn't the easiest kid to raise. I did a lot of dumb stuff, and trusting an outsider isn't my strong suit. A beautiful woman shows up here with do-gooder written all over her, and I go into protective mode. Yes. Sister Elena raised me. But my family really was from Missouri, and they were good people, I'm told. I like that part of my life. Some of the other parts, not so much."

"Guess you're allowed a few secrets." She timidly slipped her arm through his. "Thanks for telling me."

"So, what about you? Any secrets you'd like to share?"

"No. I think I told you my whole bag of bad decisions."

Her touch felt as if she drew him closer, making him

withdraw his hand from his pocket to take her arm carefully. The idea she had just flat-out lied to him didn't seem to matter. Was that her plan all along?

"Shouldn't we get going?" she asked softly.

Her touch was light against his arm as he slid his hand around hers. They dodged a few motorcycles crossing the street and moved down a boardwalk toward the beach when Axel spotted them. Mr. and Mrs. Who-Are-They. They lifted a hand in greeting, and Meredith quickly responded in kind. This was an odd place for them to be at this time of evening. Off the beaten path didn't strike him like their type of place. Although dressed casually, they moved like two people with an objective, not just a stroll on the beach.

"We keep bumping into you," the man said, making direct eye contact with Axel. That spoke volumes, especially when the woman made a classic security scan around them.

"Isn't this place amazing?" the wife asked Meredith. "I love how it's so friendly, and hardly any tourists."

"Me, too," Meredith responded. "How did you decide to come here?"

"Word of mouth," the husband quickly answered. "We wanted to be alone with a more romantic feel than a big resort." He slipped an arm around his trophy wife's shoulders then kissed her cheek. "Right, hon?"

She sent him a loving glance and hugged his arm. "You were so right about this place."

The man was a little more fit than he once thought. Although the pretend wife was attractive, up close, she had a steely eyed glint and a sharp angled face. In Hollywood, the woman would have been perfect for an action movie hero who could easily take out a terrorist cell. These two were not newlyweds. He had the protection business written all over him.

"Where are you from?" Axel asked casually.

"Chicago. Thought this would be a nice time of year to leave all the bad weather behind."

"Flew to Vegas to get married then here." She laid a hand on his chest and batted her eyes with a bit of tease at her partner.

"Where you guys headed?" the man asked with a friendly grin plastered on his face.

"Just a stroll on the beach," Axel said and proceeded to take a step in that direction before Meredith could add more information. "We'd better get going. Have a nice evening. And congratulations."

The man blinked at the sudden dismissal and stepped back so they could pass. Axel hurried to the beach where they both removed their shoes to walk on the warm sand. "I didn't get their names. Do you know?"

She shook her head. "No. Never thought to ask. Guess I should have introduced myself since we arrived on the same plane."

Axel continued to hold Meredith's hand and decided to forget the mysterious couple for the moment. "It's just a short walk from here."

The twilight breezes moved her hair and toyed with the hem of her dress. Stealing glances at her profile, he decided he enjoyed how she continually studied the sea as if lost in a memory. He couldn't interrupt much in the fading light, causing him to wonder if she waited for something or someone.

Music, happy voices, and bells attached with rides, games, and other festival noises reached their ears. Darkness reached completeness as the infectious dance of tropical gaiety mixed with the children yelling to them as they approached. The twins jumped up and down with excitement as they entered the festival grounds.

Between the turtle races, ring toss games, Ferris-wheel, and other stomach-bouncing rides, the evening progressed more quickly than Axel thought possible. The twins appeared to be 100 percent again, and none of the other children had come down with similar symptoms. Rosa tried her best to monopolize Meredith's time and attention, but Pedro didn't appear to mind since he clung to Axel most of the evening.

Each child was treated to a tasty dessert cake. Axel knew this would take a bite out of the food budget until Sister Elena told him where the money had come from.

"That sweet Meredith donated one hundred dollars for the children tonight. Said it was her souvenir memory," she sighed. "I think that means she's leaving soon."

Axel listened as he observed Meredith take turns dancing with the children. Her laughter hit him hard, thinking she might leave. Whatever she'd done in the States could have been her survival ticket. He'd known lots of men who had done the wrong thing for the right reason. Why couldn't a woman do the same thing?

"Time to go, children," Sister Elena called as she clapped her hands. Like baby chicks, they hurried to surround her. "Luis went to get our shuttle. Follow me."

Meredith got in line holding the hands of the twins. "You two look sleepy."

"Come with us." It was Rosa.

"Tuck me in, Meredith." The little boy laid his head against her hip.

She swallowed hard and bent down to kiss the top of his head. "I will. Be a good boy and do as Sister Elena tells you. Be a big help. I'll be there soon."

"Nonsense," the sister said with a wave of the hand. "I have two volunteers waiting for us. You two need to dance without us. See? It is couples' time now." She pointed to the dance floor. "Axel, show this woman some Belize hospitality."

"Oh, that's okay, Sister, I—"

"Go," she demanded as Axel pulled her away from the children.

"I'll be there soon." Meredith waved goodbye.

"Maybe yes. Maybe no." She winked at Axel. "Go," she repeated.

Axel reached for her hand and pulled her onto the dance floor where a slow melody drifted into the night. Couples embraced and whispered into each other's ears or stole a kiss from one another. The longer the music played, the closer he managed to pull her against his body. They swayed together as if one, and their faces pressed together. His hands circled her waist as her arms went around his neck. No words passed between them as their steps slowed and the press of their bodies hinted at needs long suppressed from lack of trust.

He navigated her to the edge of the dance floor then led her down to the sandy beach. The lapping waves drew them closer as they continued to hold hands. The moon rose in the night sky, spilling a trail of light across the water. Music still drifted on the breeze toward them as the rustle of palms teased their senses with the perfume of flowers.

"Do you ever get used to this place? I mean the beauty. The serenity?" Meredith turned toward him, a breath away.

"I thought I had until you showed up. I'm seeing it with new eyes."

He wanted to say the right thing, words that wouldn't scare her or force a retreat. The moonlight touched her face and gave him courage to pull her into his arms.

"Axel…" she whispered. Staring at his mouth, her lips parted as she let her eyes look into his. Words were no longer needed when he lowered his head and captured her mouth. For the first time, maybe since forever, he felt whole and alive.

His hands went up to her hair then he kissed her again, this time longer, spilling the desires he'd held in check when he saw her earlier in the evening. The hunger in her response may have been loneliness or the need for something she could count on. Whatever the reason, he wanted to be a part of the solution, not the problem.

When their kiss released, Axel wondered if he appeared as startled at the sudden passion as Meredith's face showed. At the same time he gathered her into his embrace, he spotted them; Mr. and Mrs. Perfect standing on the edge of the dance floor, searching the darkness.

<h1 style="text-align:center">CHAPTER 12</h1>

Walking back by way of the beach, Meredith let the sounds of the steel drums and maracas lift her spirits. Meredith didn't want to evaluate the storm of heat and passion that had overwhelmed both of them by surprise. The rush of falling in love wasn't anything she ever wanted to forget. Nothing had ever taken her to that place where she craved the feel of another's strength and desire for her. The touch of his hands in her hair as he captured her mouth melted any resistance and fear she had for a man she barely knew.

Even now, as they walked along the water's edge, he stopped and swung her around as she experienced what felt like pure joy. Lifting her into his arms, he kissed her again and she surrendered to his touch. An impatient eagerness to have more of him coaxed her willingness to also touch him in a way that kindled a growing flame between them. Before they continued to the orphanage, Axel helped her up onto the boardwalk then admired her without hesitation, causing a wave of joy to swell inside her.

"This isn't how I expected the evening to go." His arms went around her and pulled her forward off the boardwalk so she slid down into his arms once more. He buried his lips against her naked shoulders and neck. Slowly, he took a step back, leaving her a little dazed but satisfied. "Maybe I should slow down."

"Yes. I think you should," she said, slipping her arms around him then tugged him closer. Standing on tiptoe, she kissed his neck and tightened her embrace. "Oh. You mean both of us," she said coyly.

He pulled her after him onto the boardwalk, laughing. Walking arm in arm, enjoying the rustle of palms on a tropical evening, they soon found themselves back at the orphanage. Meredith was surprised at her own laughter as they entered the gathering room and were met by a frowning Sister Elena.

"What's wrong?" A wave of panic washed over Meredith as she pivoted toward the stairs. "Are the children okay?"

"Yes. Yes. They are waiting for you to say good night." Then she leveled a contemptuous glare at Axel. "I need to talk to you. Now." She turned and walked toward the dining room.

He shrugged at Meredith. "Go ahead and say good night. I'll walk you home."

Even as she reached the top of the stairs, Sister Elena's angry voice reached her. Axel's response was notably stern without being loud. Maybe he was gone too long or her medical services were required. She recognized what a job here could really mean. She'd witnessed plenty of medical professionals burnout because of time constraints and lack of time to have a normal life. Was that what she wanted?

Walking into the girls' room, she saw little bodies sit up in bed, in the glow of a night-light. They each required a kiss and to be tucked in. Then she noticed Rosa was missing.

"Rosa is hiding. She wants you to find her," a small voice admitted.

"Where is she hiding?" Meredith asked in a loud whisper.

They pointed to a place outside their room. She hurried to the boys' room where the story was the same. Pedro was hiding, and they wanted to be tucked in before telling her where he was. Once more, they pointed outside their room with yawns that muffled their words.

Stepping outside their room, she spotted them peeking through the railing to the area below. When she walked up behind them, they turned around slowly and reached for her with the saddest little faces she'd ever seen.

"Now that you two are all better, I think Sister Elena expects you to sleep in your assigned beds. You can't keep doing this. It's been almost a week. Come on. I'll tuck you in." They yawned at the same time.

"Sister Elena is mad at Axel. She is fussing at him," Pedro said, pointing to the stairs.

"Sometimes grown-ups' fuss, but the next day all is well. You'll see. Sister Elena loves Axel."

"If you would be our mommy, Axel could marry you, and he could be our daddy," Rosa said, entering her room.

"I think we should talk about this after you have a

good night's sleep. Okay?"

They agreed and returned to their designated rooms. It didn't take long for them to fall asleep in their own beds. She waited to make sure they weren't faking it. Tiptoeing out in the hallway, she closed the bedroom doors and gave a thumbs-up to the volunteer who planned to stay the night in the little room separating the children. A wave of satisfaction came over her, knowing she'd made a difference in at least two little lives.

Slipping down the stairs, she found her way to the gathering room and was nearly mowed down by a dark-haired beauty in skin-tight pants and a tube top. Her spike heels clicked on the tile floor as she breezed past Meredith.

"Axel," she snapped in a sultry Southern voice.

Meredith watched him turn as if in slow motion toward the approaching woman who picked up speed. Before he could respond, the woman threw herself into his arms and kissed him so hard on the mouth, Meredith felt a sense of embarrassment for Sister Elena whose face had turned red.

"I've missed you," she said, running her fingers through his hair. "Well, aren't you glad to see me?" She didn't wait for an answer but moved to Sister Elena and kissed her on the cheek. "Sister Elena, you are looking—fit."

What was happening? Who was this woman? The beauty pivoted toward Meredith as she approached the three. She opened her mouth to introduce herself but was cut off.

"Oh. I see you've hired more help. Good." The woman looked back at Axel who had turned a shade of rage that scared her even from this distance. Before Axel could respond, the beauty continued. "Be a lamb, will you, and get me some bottled water. I'm parched." She then proceeded to wrap her arms around Axel's neck and toy with his hair with her index finger. When Meredith didn't respond, the woman turned an impatient stare toward Meredith that would have melted iron. "Do you not understand English?"

Axel peeled her off him and pulled back his shoulders. "Sonya, this is Meredith Marshall. She's a nurse practitioner from the States. She's helping out here a few days. Meredith this is Sonya Lavenworth."

She couldn't believe it. This was an up-close-and-personal, real-life movie star. To top it off, she was hanging all over the man Meredith had planned to take back to her room and see how the night unfolded. "Nice to meet you," Meredith said quietly, wondering if she should offer her hand in friendship. Truth be told, her first inclination was to check her appearance in the mirror since this creature with the flawless complexion and million-dollar smile made her feel like Mrs. Potts from Beauty and the Beast.

"Hello," Sonya cooed, eyeing Meredith from head to toe.

The beautiful new dress she'd spent almost forty dollars on, a fortune right now, compared to the chic outfit Sonya wore, might leave the impression she purchased it at a resale shop. Sonya arched one eyebrow, while the corner of her wide mouth lifted in a haughty smirk. Once more, she forced her arm around Axel's neck without breaking eye contact with Meredith. Every woman knew the marking-my-territory move.

"How long will you be here?" she asked Meredith.

"Not long," she said, shifting her attention to Axel who wore the expression of a man caught between two lovers.

"Pity. I was going to invite you to our wedding." She reached out her free arm to Sister Elena. "Do you think the children would like to be in the wedding?"

"I doubt it is possible," she snapped, obstinate chin rising in disapproval.

"Oh well. They are a rowdy bunch," she said with pouty lips then kissed Axel on the edge of his mouth. "I'm finally done filming for the next few months, and I thought this would be a great time for us to move forward, Axel." She turned an icy contempt on the competition. "You know, like we planned." She held out her hand for everyone to see her engagement ring.

Axel once more removed her arm, and this time clamped down on her hand hard enough, she winced. "Let's talk about this later, Sonya."

"On your boat, I hope. I did make reservations at that quaint little hole in the wall if you'd rather stay at a hotel tonight."

Meredith had had enough. "Sister Elena, I'm going to head back to the hotel. The children are tucked in, and no one seems to have come down with what the twins had. I'll drop by tomorrow to double-check on them."

"I'll walk you out," the sister said, moving in her direction.

"No. Please. You've had a busy day, too. I'll walk or catch one of those bicycle taxis to go back to"—she sent a bland glance toward the movie star— "the cute hole-in-the-wall hotel."

Axel pushed Sonya aside and stepped toward her. "You shouldn't walk back alone. It's mostly safe, but you never know. Luis is just leaving. He can take you."

She pulled her shoulders back and stared him straight in his baby blues, cringing at the thought of how she'd acted like a lovesick fool all evening.

"I'm a big girl, Axel. I can manage on my own. But, thanks." Pivoting, she marched out the door and down the steps, head held high, with all the grace and composure she could muster. When she turned toward her hotel, she noticed he continued to stand in the doorway. Almost instantly, another silhouette appeared, leaning into him. Sonya.

She didn't waste time on her walk back to the hotel. In spite of various cafes and shops still open or just closing, it was darker than she'd imagined it would be. One or two people recognized her as the new clinic doctor and waved. She'd never quite convinced the patients she wasn't a doctor. But knowing others continued to visit on the street gave her confidence to proceed by herself.

"I think you are being followed, Miss Doctor Lady." Luis stopped his vehicle alongside her. "Please. Axel wanted me to drive you to the hotel." He took a quick scan of the street and back toward the boardwalk.

A wave of relief washed over her at seeing him. Climbing in, she exhaled as if the weight of the world were on her shoulders. "Thanks, Luis." This time she looked back toward the boardwalk where several people were leaving the beach. "I didn't notice anyone following me."

He chuckled. "I said that because Axel thought you might refuse my offer. I tricked you."

"You sure did. I appreciate your effort." A burst of laughter beat the heck out of having an ugly cry.

"It is on my way. Axel is very upset." He pulled cautiously onto the street, even though there were few cars at this hour. "He is angry at Miss Sonya."

"Engaged?" she breathed incredulously.

He shrugged. "I didn't know. She has come before but did not stay long. Sister Elena says she doesn't like the children, so she doesn't have much time for her. I could tell the good sister was irritated after coming home from the festival. She got a phone call from that woman. This sent the sister into a fizz. You know. Mixed up."

"A fizz. Yes. I understand."

Luis shook his head. "Those Hollywood people are different from us." Meredith liked that he was including her in his group. "Axel escaped that place. He's a good man."

"I guess that's where they met."

"Yes. She was a guest on his show."

"Show? Axel had a show?"

"Oh yes. He was very popular for maybe eight years. You didn't know?"

The fog lifted. No wonder he seemed familiar. He was Axel Cahill, Surviving the Wild. Not only did he have a regular cable and YouTube show on how to survive dangerous situations in the outdoors, but another show that took celebrities out to the back end of nowhere. He would put them in peril and show them how to make it out alive.

"I thought you said he left all that behind."

"He did. Still gets paid the royalties from the show. Most of the money he gives to Sister Elena for the children or uses for repairs. For a while, he worked as a stunt double, and even now helps as an advisor on some of those big action-adventure movies when he is short of cash. Depends on if Sister Elena or the children need something he can't pay for right away." Luis pulled up in front of the hotel. "He is a good man. I hope he won't leave us for that woman. She thinks she's better than us. We are pretty simple." Meredith unfastened her seat belt when he tapped her on the arm. "But you belong here. We like you."

She patted his hand on the steering wheel. "Thanks, Luis. Did Sister Elena put you up to that?"

"Maybe." He shrugged innocently. "But it is true. Axel has been happy with you here. Not so much the last year. We all have secrets."

She wondered if he was talking about her or Axel.

She waved goodbye and climbed the steps. As she entered the lobby, the couple from the plane, Mr. and Mrs. Perfect as Axel called them, stepped out to cut off her retreat to her room.

"We've been waiting for you," the man confessed.

CHAPTER 13

For some reason, Meredith had never formally introduced herself to the couple, and Axel had not bothered to ask, either. She remembered now, he had actually bristled a bit and hurried her along when they encountered them. Did he think they were suspicious, or was he in a hurry to romance her? In spite of being strangers, right this minute, Mrs. Perfect felt like the only person she knew well enough to trust.

She'd stepped out with her husband and wore a frown. "We saw you walking alone when we passed you in a taxi. Then an old truck stopped and picked you up." She laid a hand over her heart. "I was afraid something was wrong. It's kind of a sketchy place after dark. We were just about ready to contact the police." Reaching out, the woman touched her arm lightly. "Are you all right?"

"Yes. Yes. Thank you. A friend picked me up. He works at the orphanage. Sister Elena sent him after me when I started back alone."

"That's wise she did that for you, especially at

night," Mr. Perfect spoke. "Where's your boyfriend? I thought he seemed like the type who would bring you home."

With the last comment, she burst into tears and walked away. She heard the woman reprimand her husband and run to catch up with her.

"I'm sorry about that. He's all macho with a Great Pyrenees mentality."

"Pyrenees mentality?" She sniffed.

"They're range dogs. They circle the pasture and let the sheep have freedom. He's alert for problems like coyotes. When necessary, he runs them off." Her voice sounded encouraging. "I was raised on a farm. I know I don't look like it."

"I'm sorry. I'm Meredith Marshall."

"Tammy Flynn. Well, it is now that I married Lester."

He joined them and apologized for his comments. "Sweetie, this is Meredith. Why don't you go get us a class of wine."

"I just want to go to bed." Meredith sniffed again, afraid she'd lose all control.

"Come on. A little girl talk will make it better. Are you afraid?"

Meredith nodded, thinking Axel might come try and apologize or pick up where he'd left off. She could still remember how he felt when he kissed her. The thought she'd allowed herself to fall for such a playboy sickened her. "I don't want to talk to the man I was with."

"You girls talk. I'll stay out here and keep a lookout. If you don't want to talk to him, I'll insist he leave."

"Thank you. I just am not interested in anything he

has to say tonight, Lester."

His eyebrows raised as he shifted his attention to his wife.

Meredith continued, "Tammy told me your name. I'm Meredith, by the way. Guess since we keep bumping into each other, you should know my name."

"Right. Meredith, I'll make sure you ladies can have some girl talk. I'll be right over there if you need me."

"Come on," Tammy said, looping her arm through hers and tugged her toward the bar area. "A glass of wine will do you good. My treat."

Meredith let herself be led to the Caribbean-themed bar where reggae music softly played in the background. Candlelight beamed through unmatched jars on the table and artificial torches with flickering lights kept the atmosphere cozy. There was an outdoor patio surrounded by tropical vegetation that normally would have drawn Meredith outdoors, but she didn't want to have any encounters with Axel if he came.

On the other hand, why would he come to see her now that the beautiful fiancée had arrived? He could torture her with his rogue good looks and charm. The woman had flown from who knows where to be with him during her time off. Maybe the aloof greeting he gave her was some kind of turn-on they had going on between them. The engagement ring was quite a rock and must have cost a small fortune.

She glanced down at where her wedding band had rested, noticing the once crease of its existence had disappeared. Even while separated from her ex, the wedding band remained in place, in her hopes that someday things would change. But it got worse. Drugs. Gambling. Borrowing money he couldn't pay back.

Agreeing to do things to pay down their debt that were shady at best. Jeopardizing a good job. Finally, she had to get out. He wouldn't get help because he didn't have a problem. According to him, she was the problem.

After every fight, he'd apologize and begged for her forgiveness and say she was the best part of his life. Gradually, he became physically abusive. At first, it was a shove or a twisted arm. Slowly it turned into more visible abuse until her girlfriends insisted she needed to leave him. They'd rallied around her, protected her, and helped her move forward. For that, she'd always be grateful. Her team at the hospital was understanding and let her take time to put her life in order. She could only imagine how she had worried them after disappearing. Soon, she'd be able to tell them the whole story.

The next nail in their marital coffin was when the bank notified her about her car being repossessed. She'd learned the mortgage had gone unpaid for six months and no taxes paid in two years. Why had she agreed to letting him be in charge of the finances? Even her electric had been disconnected. He didn't care since he wasn't living there and agreed to transferring everything into her name. That's when she'd had enough. Moving into an apartment, buying a used car from a friend, and starting over wasn't a chore. It was a breath of fresh air.

She brought her aunt, who'd raised her, to live with her since she was in failing health. It wasn't until she died that she found out there was a life insurance policy for two hundred thousand dollars. Nathan had come to her side, like always, and put on a show of being a supportive ex-husband. Her aunt's lawyer invited him to the reading of the will, since he was also named. Needless to say, he put on his best mourning face until he learned he'd only received a run-down piece of property. On the other hand, when she was given the check for two hundred thousand dollars and her aunt's ten-acre farm, he lit up like a Christmas tree.

The divorce wasn't final, so he made an effort to get his fair share. The judge ruled otherwise. When he confessed to her he needed money to pay off his gambling debt to the Russian mob who had been financing his habit, she refused.

He even had the audacity to bring two of his Russian mob gate-keepers to the hospital for an introduction. They listened to him threaten her and explain how much trouble he was in and if she didn't come through for him, he would be toast. They pressed a business card into her palm before leaving but remained solemn and unaffected by Nathan's predicament.

That night, he came to her apartment again to beg for money. And just like the last time, she refused. He exploded. This time, he hit her.

Then the most amazing thing happened.

~ ~ ~ ~

Midnight. What a disaster the evening had turned out to be. It had held so much promise then the bane of his existence arrived at the orphanage. After their last encounter, he finally understood Sonya Lavenworth was one of the many things wrong in his life, and she occupied the top of the list.

He'd been taken in by her beauty and notoriety as he made climbing the popularity ladder in Hollywood a breeze. It was almost too late when he came to grips with how toxic the woman was to his mental state and overall well-being. Of course, rejecting her was like giving your misbehaved feline an abundance of catnip. The more you mistreated, ignored, or rejected her, the more determined she became to seduce you into compliance.

Now here he was, once more, in her emotional crosshairs, when all he wanted to do was walk on the beach and get to know Meredith Marshall. What was it about dangerous women that drew him in? Did he have a death wish? Where Sonya had sharp claws and enjoyed ripping a man's heart and mental state to shreds, Meredith wore velvet gloves and secrets to hide behind. And hiding wasn't working for him.

Running up the steps of the hotel into the lobby, it was obvious by the emptiness of the room, most tourists had called it a night. In spite of being a Friday night and festival weekend, the locals would be partying other places than the tourist section of Turtle Bay. He hustled toward the check-in desk when Mr. Perfect came out from behind a large potted palm. His body went on alert at the sudden appearance of the man who now had lost his pleasant, irritating smile.

"Kind of late to see you here," he said, narrowing one eye at Axel.

Confrontation. Axel normally would not take lightly to the stance or the tone of voice, which meant the guy had an agenda. Given the way his jaw tightened and released and his lips thinned, this guy wasn't in a positive mood. Good. Neither was he. Macho nonsense was only going to make getting to Meredith a tricky endeavor.

"Shouldn't you be honeymooning or something?" Axel sighed as he felt his fists double in frustration.

"I think we both know we're not honeymooning, Mr. Cahill."

Axel's whole body triggered to alert mode.

"After all, you did a pretty good job of going through our room the other night. Guess you missed the camera I installed."

"Get out of my way." Axel spoke through gritted teeth and tried to step around the man who was nearly as tall as himself. But he anticipated the move and blocked Axel again. "Do you have something to say to me, or are you just being really annoying?"

"If you're here to speak to the lady, she doesn't want to talk to you," he said with a smirk.

"And how would you know that?" Axel spotted Meredith in the bar talking with Mrs. Perfect. She caught sight of him and rose to her feet with Mrs. Perfect glancing over her shoulder at him. He moved in that direction, only to be cut off again. "Look. This is none of your business, and I'd appreciate it if you stopped doing whatever this is."

Lester jammed a finger in Axel's chest. "Well, I'm making it my business."

In a quick reaction to a threat, Axel grabbed his finger and twisted it, bringing the man to his knees, just as it snapped. The man cried out as his knees slammed against the tile floor. Axel became aware of the sudden chaos unfolding, involving a call for security and a few gasps from tourists, even as he pushed Mr. Perfect over backward and stepped over him. "Stay out of my way," he growled.

Meredith hurried out of the bar with Mrs. Perfect

coming to the rescue of her pretend husband. Security, two big off-duty policemen, a head taller than him with about twenty-five more pounds of muscle, grabbed him and slammed him down in one of the lobby chairs. They ordered him to stay put, but, as soon as they went to help the man off the floor, he headed down the hall to Meredith's room.

"Meredith, wait," he called but she slammed the door and locked it. This only managed to scare her back to where she was a few days earlier. In his calmest voice, he tried to reach out to her. "Let me explain. Sonya is my past. I—"

He felt the grip of security on each of his arms as they dragged him backward toward the lobby.

CHAPTER 14

Meredith double-checked the French doors to the patio outside her room before pulling the bamboo shades. Seeing Axel drop Lester to the floor like he was a rag doll retrieved the memory of how her ex had used her as a punching bag when she wouldn't bail him out of trouble one more time. He wasn't nearly as fit as Axel and, from what she just witnessed, no one got in his way.

So much for the strong quiet type she mistook him for.

So much for the tropical romance she hoped was blooming.

So much for new sensations at the touch of his lips and hands to her body.

So much for starting over in paradise.

So much for feeling like she deserved a chance at a family.

A tap at the door ended the pity party. She shook it off and peeked through the peephole to recognize Tammy. Cautiously, she cracked the door open enough to see worry lines along her forehead.

"The police took that guy away, Meredith. He hurt Lester. Could you come check him out before they call in an ambulance from the resort down the beach?"

"Let me get my backpack. I carry some supplies in there for emergencies." In seconds, she'd followed Tammy down to the lobby, where hotel personnel, a security guard, and a police officer helped Lester to a chair. She didn't spot any blood, but the man was ashen. "Lester, I'm so sorry this happened to you. Let me do a quick exam."

The voices around her were explaining what they saw, mixed with what they thought they saw, go down between the two men. The policeman took notes, the names of witnesses, and then took Tammy aside to fill in the blanks.

Meredith squatted on the floor next to Lester's chair and took his hand in hers. After a few seconds, she noticed his frown. He wasn't complaining like her ex would have done. Of course, he'd be wanting to sue someone for attacking him, even if he deserved it. What had Lester done to cause such a reaction from Axel? He didn't strike her as a violent man. Protective, yes, especially of little children and Sister Elena.

"Lester, your finger is broken. Normally I would take an X-ray to be sure, but as you can see it's a bit misshaped."

"Can you fix it?"

"I think I can put it back in place, but you really need to see a doctor. I don't think it will require surgery."

"Surgery? It's just a little break on my finger," he said impatiently.

"Yes, that is kind of true. But you'll probably need a splint to protect it from further injury. It will help it heal properly. I have splinted fingers next to the fractured one to add support."

"Then do that."

She nodded and asked about his knees. "Maybe we should go to your room so Tammy can help remove your pants for me to examine you." He rolled his eyes in frustration and nodded compliance. She turned to the desk clerk. "I need a chair on wheels or a wheelchair if there is one. I don't want him walking until I've examined him."

"Miss Marshall, I need to speak to you when you can find a few minutes." It was the policeman. He was an older gentleman who had taken to yawning even during the excitement going on around him. "Should I wait for you, or would you drop by the station in the morning?"

"In the morning might be better. I don't know what I'm dealing with Mr. Flynn."

He tucked his notepad in his shirt pocket and appeared relieved. "If I'm not there, you can speak to anyone. Just tell them your name."

"Meredith," Tammy called as they were wheeling Lester down the hall in a desk chair.

She grabbed her backpack and ran to walk alongside them. It reminded her of being in the ER again. Between working on the pediatric floor and the ER, her life had become chaotic. But it was better than facing the truth outside of work. Besides, she needed the money to get her life on track.

Then an unexpected event changed everything.

Before she could go down memory lane, Tammy

was ushered into the room where one of the security guards lifted Lester to sit on the edge of the bed.

"You guys can wait in the hall. Tammy, can you help Lester out of those slacks?" Meredith caught an exchange of frustrated looks between them, even though Lester smiled wolfishly.

"Yes, sweetheart. I don't think I can manage."

"You're a big baby, you know that?" she said sweetly, but Meredith noticed her expression was dark with a frown, reflecting a less-than-worried vibe about her husband. "He has a robe in the closet, Meredith. Can you get it for me?"

She nodded then hurried to the closet and moved hangers to reach the terrycloth robe. Something leathery and hard touched her fingers as she moved a jacket. Underneath the garment was a holster and handgun. Slipping her hand into the pocket, with a few papers, she found a picture of herself. Her heart raced as she jammed it back into the pocket.

"Meredith?" Lester called.

"Coming," she said, pulling the robe free and hurrying back to his side. He lay prone on the bed in his boxers. Tammy stood back with her arms crossed as if she was irritated instead of sitting next to her husband or at least standing next to the bed. "Let me have a look at those knees," she said, first offering the robe to Tammy. When she waved her off, Meredith covered him from the thigh and across his lower extremities.

"She's a little shy." He winked at his wife.

Something was wrong in that relationship and here she had just spilled her guts to the woman through a flood of tears. Could no one be trusted?

She put him through a few paces to evaluate whether

anything was bad enough to go to the hospital. "Lester, I can't be sure anything is seriously wrong here, either. But since you were able to bend your knee, and I didn't hear any popping noises, I'm guessing you are going to be really sore. There might be some swelling. The bruising has started. I'll see if the pharmacy has a cane they can send over, or maybe the hotel has one. Those tiles are pretty hard to bang your knee on."

"Got that right," he said, sitting up with her help. He slipped on the robe and tried to stand, only to sit right back down. "That smarts."

"If you have some acetaminophen, I'd take it for pain every four hours. I'm sorry this happened to you because of me. What happened?"

"Your boyfriend—"

"He's not my boyfriend. We met the day we arrived. He works at the orphanage where I've been helping out." She sounded a little more insistent than she meant. "Sorry. He works there is all."

Lester arched an eyebrow and continued. "Yeah, well, he was determined to find you. I told him you weren't interested in seeing him and to move along. He took offense at that, and this happened."

Meredith pinched the bridge of her nose and shook her head. "Did he say what he wanted?"

"No. Better stay away from him. I've seen that type before. They're hotheads and big trouble, especially around women."

Tammy stepped forward; her expression softened. "He's right, Meredith. I think he'll cool his heels in jail tonight, so nothing to worry about. But if you'd like for me to stay with—"

"No. I think I just want to go to bed."

"I know what you mean," Lester said, glancing toward his wife.

She ignored him and walked Meredith to her room. "Thank you for helping out. I'm glad we don't need to go to the clinic near the resort."

"It's been all about me tonight. I never asked what your husband or you do for a living." She thought of the gun she'd found in the closet and her picture.

"I was a model for Charmed Cosmetics when I met Lester. He is an independent contractor for something." She put her finger to her cheek and appeared confused. "I forget for what."

For the first time, she could tell the woman was definitely acting. Whatever the reason, it was none of her business, and she didn't care if the two were having an affair, international spies, hiding from the law, or unscrupulous entrepreneurs. Albeit suspicious, they'd done her a favor getting rid of Axel.

Why did he want to see her anyway? That much she wanted to know. Also, where did the Flynns get a picture of her and for what? Maybe she was mistaken. After all, it was dark in the closet. She was high on adrenaline and had just seen the gun.

"See you in the morning. If you need anything at all, you can call the room phone or our cell phone." She jotted down two sets of numbers. "Okay?" she said, touching Meredith's arm tenderly.

"I appreciate that. Lester may need help walking tomorrow. Those knees will be sore in the morning. Encourage him to use a cane."

"I'm not sure I'll have much luck with that. He's pretty proud and likes to be in charge. Bless his heart." She frowned then batted her eyes like a baby doll.

The two parted after a few awkward comments about Lester. Meredith suspected it was one more thing to throw her off-balance and soften the evening's events.

In spite of the unexpected disappointments, both in her ability to make good decisions and make friends with normal people, a hot shower did wonders. The bed was cool, and the ceiling fan made a soft clicking sound that lulled her to sleep. Her last thoughts were of the children at the orphanage. They were the good in this hellish night. She let the images of the twins dance in her head as sleep took her away.

CHAPTER 15

The weather had turned ominous. The breeze had intensified to a gale, and the once-blue sky was now blanketed with rolling dark clouds. Waves crashed ashore and a red flag warning was given to her when she stopped in the coffee shop.

"Tropical storm brewing. Not named yet but it's expected. With any luck, it will turn north and hit Texas instead of us. "So, stay out of the water. Those waves are mean today."

"Thanks. Should I be doing something to prepare?" She felt a twinge of anxiety knowing that this was going to delay her exit from the little town.

"Nah. Day or so out, but Sister Elena always says prayers are a good idea."

Meredith smiled at the thought of her giving orders for everyone to get down on their knees and pray this thing away. "I will keep that in mind." She lifted her disposable cup in a salute of approval. After asking for directions to the police station, she walked outside the hotel.

She hailed a bicycle taxi and sipped her dark brew after giving a destination to the driver. In spite of the lack of a beautiful tropical day, the anticipation of a storm fit her mood better. Part of her had always loved rainy days and taken them as an opportunity to slow down. Growing up, her aunt would open the windows of her house to air it out during a storm. Said it just made the house smell better. They would read, make soup, and sometimes enjoy a movie. Today, she missed her. Maybe a storm would wash away her anger, clearing a brain path to figure out where she should hide next.

The police station was at the end of a street several blocks west of the beach. The two police cars parked out front were at least twenty years old but shone like a new penny. In the States, they would be featured at car shows. Here, they were a working necessity. The building reminded her of something from a bygone era, but inside it was clean and void of any old-fashioned atmosphere. The modern amenities of computers, smart boards, and furniture, although sparse, was impressive for such a small operation.

"Can I help you, ma'am?" asked an older gentleman with a bald head and wide nose. "You lost?"

She told him who she was and about the request for her to appear. He grinned and waved her off. "Oh yeah. Heard all about it. That Axel," he laughed, "must have really wanted to talk to you. He told us all about how that creep kept following you around, and he had been making sure you were safe."

"Making sure I was safe?" she said in bewilderment.

"We're trying to find out more about him since Axel had no luck."

"Are you telling me the Flynns are suspects in something?" Somehow, she wasn't surprised. The gun. Her picture. At least she hadn't imagined that.

"No. No. We're following up on Mr. Flynn who filed a complaint and pressed charges. Folks at the hotel called and said he's hobbling around pretty good. That pretty wife of his doesn't seem too concerned about his welfare. Called him a big baby loud enough everyone could hear. Got into a little heated argument over something as they were leaving. Ahh. Marital bliss." He continued to display a big toothy smile. "Don't miss it."

"Me, either," she said flippantly. "So, I guess you don't need anything from me after all?"

He grabbed a form from underneath the counter and shoved it across the surface to her. "Just fill this out about what you saw and how things went down. We pretty much already know since there were plenty of witnesses. We basically need to know if you were expecting Axel—" He shrugged. "Oh, you know. Your side of the story. Axel already told us his side. That's good enough for us."

"What?" she said incredulously. "He's gone? I thought you locked him up."

"Well, he spent the night here so we could do due diligence. Didn't actually lock him up. He's a pretty nice guy. Played dominoes for a while."

"Dominoes?"

"We learned a long time ago not to play cards with him. He always wins. I, for one, think he cheats." His big eyes got rounder and wider at the confession. "But don't tell him you heard it from me."

"Why would I tell him?"

"Heard he was kinda sweet on you. He's a loner, so

when some of the locals saw him with you, we figured—"

"You figured wrong. We just met almost two weeks ago."

"Whatever you say, miss. Anyway, he slept here the rest of the night in one of our cells. Don't worry. We didn't lock him up or anything like that. Sister Elena came this morning and promised to bring some bail money when she gets a few extra dollars." He rolled his eyes upward. "Like that will ever happen. That orphanage place is hanging on by a thread."

"What if I pay the bail?"

The officer raised his eyebrows in surprise.

"I don't want Sister Elena to have to clean up Axel's mess, especially if it was because of me." She filled out the summary part of the paperwork then glanced at the officer. "Well? How much?"

"I'll find out."

He disappeared into an office, leaving her to write a short four-sentence summary that was benign and had all the color of a piece of wet cardboard. She avoided writing down how furious she was that another woman interrupted her chance at romance and caused her to make a fast exit. Heaven forbid, she mention the dance, the kisses, the walk on the beach… She was mortified just thinking about it.

Perhaps this was a sign she shouldn't get involved with any men for a while. It wasn't going to get easier once the news got out about her and what happened several weeks before she made a beeline to the airport. It was pure luck Sister Elena was getting on the plane. She had been the one to put the thought of Belize in her head to begin with. Maybe it was one of Sister Elena's miracles.

Letting the sister believe she'd had a change of heart and wanted to visit the orphanage and future clinic only required her to make a ticket switch during a two-hour layover in Dallas. Sister Elena had no idea, especially when Meredith brought her lunch to explain her absence. There were two more stops and, finally, on the last leg of the journey, she secured a seat next to the sister.

Now that she thought about it, when did the Flynns board the plane—Dallas? She couldn't remember. The adrenaline surging through her veins that day helped to focus on an undetected escape. Everything was in place to leave. Yuri and Anton had made most of the arrangements. All she had to do was drive to a place outside of town near a little bridge over a seasonal creek. They picked her up. She left everything in the car: purse, keys, phone, and even a bag with a few groceries from a local market.

The old suitcase they brought with her things had been one of the few things of her great-aunt's she kept and stored in her tiny apartment garage. The ex left it for her and took the new pieces he'd bought for their honeymoon. The honeymoon they never took. Almost everything else had to be sold to cover bills he either neglected to pay or decided the money could be better spent on his habits. But she'd prevailed.

The officer returned with another piece of paper indicating the amount owed for Axel's bail. For a moment, she reconsidered her decision to pay for this comedy of errors, but decided in the end it was Sister Elena and the children she was helping. She hesitated giving cash, since she was going to need it soon. Taking a chance, she wrote a check on the new account she'd set up at the bank she'd chosen to help with this transition period. With any luck, she'd be long gone before anyone could trace her whereabouts.

"We don't accept checks from visitors. Sorry."

Meredith pulled out some bills, laid them down on the counter, and quickly received a receipt.

How long did she have before Nathan searched for her? And he would. In spite of the divorce, being separated for a time, and putting everything but her first in his life, he claimed to still love her. At first, she'd believed his devotion was sincere, along with his claim he was just no good for her and needed his space. Then the abuse started. At first, it was being ignored then making fun of her work, followed by shouting how stupid she was to believe this or that. At the end, before the actual divorce papers came through, he got physical. His addiction to gambling turned him into a monster.

There was a good chance he'd found out about her secret. If he had, he wasn't going to let things stand as they were. But he'd already signed the divorce decree, so there was no way he could find her treasure stashed in a bank in a little out-of-the-way town nobody ever heard of. But for the right price, anything could be discovered, and maybe even taken. Who was to say Yuri and Anton wouldn't turn on her?

~ ~ ~ ~

Axel stood on the deck of his boat and let the waves rock him as he pondered what to do first in securing the boat against the oncoming storm. Hoping it would bypass them was too carefree and unprepared for him.

He decided to secure things by letting a friend sail it to his private cove in case the storm intensified and turned in their direction. At least this distraction would mean not having to think about Sonya and her demands or the expression on Meredith's face when she saw him lip-locked with his ex-fiancée.

Lip-locked although he wanted nothing to do with Sonya Lavenworth, much less to kiss her, ever again. The mere thought of touching her made him cringe. She'd nearly destroyed him with her diva mentality and Hollywood sparkle. How could he have fallen for such a materialistic, self-centered woman? Was it her beauty? Maybe the attention she showered on him, posing for pictures when the paparazzi were around? Perhaps it masked the PTSD he still suffered from Afghanistan?

Whatever it was, the love he thought he wanted came crashing down around him when he saw her with another man, her agent. She promised it meant nothing, and it would never happen again. For a while, things felt mended, but they weren't. As he became distant, Sonya became more demanding and wanted proof of his love until she took him shopping for an engagement ring. He began slipping away to Belize—his home, his rock against insanity, until one day he just never went back.

His cell phone vibrated in his pants pocket. "Hey, buddy. What's up, Jake?" he asked his friend who knew the ins and outs of information gathering. "Got something for me?"

"Maybe. The police are now going to charge Nathan, her ex, with murder. Although he keeps saying he is innocent, that she just left town, evidence indicates otherwise. They now know he was beholden to the Russians and figures he killed her for the money. The Russians are saying they don't know anything about it because he doesn't owe them any money. We both know she settled up with them before leaving and gave them most of the rest to get her out of town."

"Why go to the trouble? There are restraining orders, security at buildings, and all that."

"My sources say it was the Russians' idea. They wanted to punish him for making them wait on their money. I have someone on the inside—"

"You what? Are you crazy?"

"All part of the job, bro. It gets better. The Russians staged her death, but she gave them the slip for some reason. Guess why?"

"No idea."

"She has tucked a large sum of money away at a bank. Word has it that it's over two million dollars. I don't know if it's stocks, bonds, annuities, or what. Not cash though."

"Where did she get that kind of money?"

"Good question. But she's been sitting on it awhile. Not sure why or how, but most everyone who knows her says she lived from paycheck to paycheck, trying to get her credit straightened out. Never went out to eat, except occasionally with a few girlfriends and, even then, she ordered soup or salad."

"How are you able to get this kind of information? Next thing you'll be telling me the name of her first dog when she was three."

"The name was Peabody, and she was four."

"Why am I not surprised? Yet you don't know where the money came from? Did she steal it? Kill someone?"

"I don't know. What I do know is Nathan is on the run. When I tapped into his phone and other technology, it appeared he's doing his own investigation on his wife."

"Ex-wife."

"Right. Speaking of which, I see here that you spent the night with a few charming locals at the police station due in part to some kind of skirmish at a hotel. Care to elaborate?"

"You're going to have to tell me how you find out all this stuff. And no, I don't care to elaborate. But the guy I had you run prints on is not the Mr. Nice Guy he pretends to be. He was waiting for me at the hotel and told me get lost and stay away from Meredith. Any chance he's working with the Russians?"

"And you, not particularity liking being told what to do, decided to make a door out of a window."

"You have such a way with words. To make a long story short, the hotel muscle intervened on his behalf. Sonya showed up last night and put a damper on getting to know Meredith better."

"The woman is toxic. I thought that was over."

"It most certainly is. She is just pretending I didn't mean it. Meredith took off, and I wanted to explain."

"Why? You find women who are trouble like a heat-seeking missile. Take it slow."

"I'm not getting involved. I just want to make sure she's not endangering the orphanage. Relax."

"If that were true, why did you go after her? I saw pictures of her, Axel. Remember? She isn't Sonya, but she is still a looker."

"That has nothing to do with it. I just want to know the kids and Sister Elena are safe."

"Well, my guess is that they aren't. So, get rid of both of those women immediately. Both are trouble. I'll keep digging. Might be a few days. I got other things I'm working on. Thinking about coming down for a visit."

"Sure. Thanks. See you soon."

"Take my advice, Axel. Find you a nice local girl who doesn't ask for much. You used to be quite the ladies' man. Maybe if you didn't sport the caveman look, you'd have better luck."

"Call when you can, Jake." Before he could offer more advice for his love life, Axel clicked off.

CHAPTER 16

The walk to the orphanage helped clear her head. Meredith detoured down the boardwalk to the beach. The crash of the waves definitely were rougher than the last couple of days. Keeping a healthy distance between her and the water still allowed some wet sand to seep between her toes. She swung her sandals in her hands and let the wind have its way with her hair.

The restaurant she'd come to love had few customers this morning. The rolling clouds appeared ominous, and the ocean didn't beckon swimmers and surfers. The boats that took tourists out to the Belize Barrier Reef were moored and being secured in case the tropical storm turned into a hurricane. She craved a cup of Juan's delicious coffee.

"Miss Meredith," Juan said as she approached. "It is good to see you so early. Would you rather sit inside where it is less windy? I have a covered patio that is protected from the wind, but the view is still excellent." He rolled his eyes toward the ocean. "Well perhaps very good. Not excellent. Besides, if it rains, you will stay dry," he said cheerfully. "Come," he said, turning and walking inside the restaurant.

He led her through the area that had been decorated in a more refined style for the higher-end customers then out to the covered patio decked with tropical palms and blooming plants that was more her style. One other person occupied the patio, a woman who talked on her cell phone.

"Can I sit over there, Juan?" She indicated a table. I think the view is better. Also, it seems the lady is taking a call. I don't want to intrude on anyone's privacy." He agreed and seated her so she faced palm trees that partially blocked the sand. In seconds, he returned with a pot of coffee and some of his hot cinnamon toast. Holding the coffee cup with both hands, she stared over the rim through the trees.

"May I join you?" came a female voice as smooth as silk.

Sonya Lavenworth. Before Meredith could even say yes, the woman pulled out a chair and sat down like it was a throne. She waved to Juan and pointed to a coffee cup on the table. He nodded and hurried off.

"I don't mean to intrude, Mary Beth—"

"It's Meredith."

"Yes, of course. I apologize."

Juan poured the star a cup of coffee and set a tin of creamer down next to the saucer.

She ignored him and glanced the other way when he said he would return with cinnamon bread. "This is a quaint little place," she sighed then took a sip of coffee like it might catch her on fire. "Have you been to the Barrier Reef Resort up the way? It is first class and has terrific restaurants and shopping. Never have to leave the grounds." She diverted her eyes toward the cup she held in her dainty hand. "The coffee is certainly much better."

"I wouldn't know," she said as Juan set some bread on the table. Meredith helped herself even as Sonya turned her nose up at it.

"I changed my plans last night and stayed in town at a little bed-and-breakfast. I went ahead and reserved it for our reunion but, apparently, Axel got into a little disagreement at the hotel."

Meredith didn't know what she expected her to say.

"About last night—I was so excited to see my Axel, I barely noticed you. I realize now I may have appeared—a bit off-putting. Axel said I was rude, so I want to apologize."

Meredith remained quiet and let her get to the point.

"Sister Elena seems quite fond of you. It was Meredith this and Meredith that, after you left. I barely had time to even talk to him for all her tongue wagging." She added enough creamer to her coffee it resembled melted marshmallows. "Pooh. Now it's cold. Could you call the waiter over to bring a hot pot?" She fingered the lace around her white blouse that slipped over one shoulder.

Meredith asked quietly if someone could bring hot coffee then addressed the actress. "Is there something you want to say to me, Ms. Lavenworth or—"

"Oh, call me Sonya," she said, patting Meredith's shoulder. "A friend of Sister Elena and my Axel's is a friend of mine."

Meredith tried to appear grateful as she forced a tight smile. "Sonya, then. Did you have something to say to me, or is this just a little get-acquainted session over coffee. It's not necessary. As you say, if you're a friend of Sister Elena's, that's good enough for me."

"And Axel? What about him?" Her face morphed into a mask of spite and contempt.

"Excuse me?"

"He seemed quite disturbed that you left and a bit irritated I had shown up unannounced."

"I only arrived maybe two weeks ago. I met Sister Elena when she was fundraising in the States. We hit it off, and she invited me to come down to take a look around, hoping I'd stay to help out at the clinic. As to Axel, he has been cordial but has been pretty clear he thinks I need to move on as soon as possible. The concern for me leaving last night so abruptly, most likely, had to do with me walking back to the hotel alone. He says it isn't safe. From what I can tell, he treats everyone in the same manner."

"I see," she said, tilting her head and searching Meredith's face as if she might find a hint of deception.

"Do you? Your tone implies you think there might be something else—maybe an attraction? There isn't."

"I'm afraid Axel and I haven't spoken this morning. After we had a"—her smile widened—"discussion about our lives together, and he got in one of his moods. You know what I mean. You must have seen him go all Rambo, like he was playing at his little television show."

"No, I'm afraid I don't know, and I've never seen his show. I figured it was fake." This time Meredith offered a snide grin. "You know, like a lot of things in Hollywood. Present company excluded, of course. As a matter of fact, he never mentioned being engaged. Not that he would have shared something like that with me."

Sonya bristled as her large eyes narrowed. "Axel can be difficult and unreasonable at times." She dabbed at her mouth with the paper napkin. "But when we make up," she said, laying her hand on her heart and rolled her eyes then exhaled with exaggeration, "it's worth it."

"Really? I find that hard to believe since you never showed up to bail him out of jail last night or even went to check on him this morning."

"And how would you know that?" she growled.

"I had to go to the station this morning because the police wanted my statement after Axel came to the hotel and got into a fight with a friend of mine. Since I was having a drink with his wife in the bar, I didn't hear the conversation. I still had to give a statement since I witnessed it, although from afar."

"Oh. Well, yes, I did know he had been arrested. The station called Sister Elena. I was still there waiting for him to return. I couldn't very well go there. If the paparazzi got wind of that, they'd be down here like a dog on a bone. My reputation is a commodity marketed to families and young adults. I can't have it tarnished by being seen going into a police station. Axel understands this."

"Yet, you let Sister Elena go there and bail him out with money she didn't have."

"I wasn't aware she had done that. It's not like she would have accepted money from me." By the tapping of her manicured nails on the tablecloth, it seemed she wasn't aware Axel had been released.

Juan came to take their order. Sonya spoke immediately, assuming he would ask her first, before he turned to Meredith.

Meredith rose and laid a twenty on the table. "I've lost my appetite, Juan." She gathered up all the snarky she could manage and raised her chin in attitude. "Enjoy your breakfast. This is one of my favorite spots. And thanks for sharing your time with me. It's been very revealing, to say the least." During the casual stroll back through the restaurant, Meredith never looked back.

Once outside, she took deep breaths and laid her hand on her heart that was going ninety to nothing. Never would she have thought of speaking that way to someone like Sonya Lavenworth. The woman was an international celebrity. Always wearing her best face. Giving to charities. Making public appearances for the troops. Cutting ribbons for cancer ward additions to hospitals that bore her name. Volunteering at soup kitchens. Political fundraisers for popular candidates.

"I'm a loser," she moaned as she ran up the steps of the orphanage. "What have I ever done?"

"You healed the sick. Just like Jesus," Sister Elena said from the porch swing. "I hope you haven't been comparing yourself to Sonya Lavenworth." She motioned for her to come sit with her.

"What a mess I caused last night. I'm sorry if I embarrassed you," she said, taking a seat next to the sister. "I was rude and very unfriendly to her and most likely did damage to Axel's relationship with her."

Sister Elena clicked her tongue at the notion then patted Meredith's leg. "We can only hope," she said flippantly.

"I just saw her at Juan's, and I was a witch. I didn't want to be, but I was petty, snarky, and condescending."

"I didn't realize you could speak her language," she said in amazement then laughed, causing Meredith to do the same. "I'm sure you were the model of civility considering she is like one of the hurricanes we have here. She blows in, stirs up some trouble, puts my Axel in turmoil, and then leaves devastation in her wake."

"You love him, don't you?"

The two women held hands.

"Yes. If I had been blessed to be a mother, I would want my child to be just like him. I'm very proud of him. Look at all this." She waved her hand around the porch and house. "Without him, we would not have a home, and the children would be out on the streets or worse. Never asks for anything and makes sure we are always taken care of. I don't know how many times he has given us his whole paycheck so that we would have enough. Or how many times he has hit his army buddies in the States up for donations. He is my angel."

"I am no such thing," Axel said, slowly walking up onto the porch. His attention went to Meredith immediately. "Can we talk?"

Sister Elena shoved at Meredith's shoulder. "Go on. I don't know what is going on between you two, but get it settled," she said forcefully.

"Yes, ma'am." Axel walked over and held his hand out. "Please, Meredith. I just want to talk."

Meredith stared at his outstretched hand and refused to take it as she stood. Those mirrored aviator sunglasses reflected her face that bore the expression of a mad pit bull. She sidestepped him and lifted her chin. "Okay. Then I need to check on the children."

"We could do that together. Neutral ground."

She liked that. It would keep the conversation light and void of harsh rhetoric. "Okay," she said so softly she could barely hear herself. The calm and unemotional man that walked beside her could have been a stranger. She guessed in some ways, he was.

What did she really know about him? Apparently, there were gaps in the things he'd shared with her. How much of it was true? It didn't matter. She wouldn't be here much longer. A walk on the beach, a dance in the moonlight with the sound of waves and Caribbean steel drums playing in the background, was nothing more than an escape from reality for a few hours. The jerk back to the here and now reminded her of the part of last night with Sonya pawing over him.

"I heard you paid my bail. Thank you," he said as they walked to the backyard. "You know Sister Elena will try and pay you back?"

"Yes."

"I'm assuming you did it so she wouldn't have to."

"Yes."

"Last night—between us…"

"It was just a dance. A kiss. This place is very romantic. Probably happens all the time."

"Not to me, it doesn't," he blurted. "You probably think I was taking advantage of you, but I—"

"Meredith. Axel." The twins came running toward them covered in wet mud, holding out their arms in excitement.

Both adults acted horrified and ran in circles away from the laughing children. More appeared, also covered in mud. Finally, several of the older ones caught Axel and Meredith then pulled them to the twins. Rosa was lifted into Axel's arms, and Meredith swung up Pedro who hugged her neck and patted her face with muddy hands.

"Pretty." He smiled then touched her windblown hair. He reached out to Axel. Rosa was reaching, too, making him step closer so they could touch each other. Instead, they grabbed a piece of clothing of the adult holding them and pulled so that Meredith and Axel faced each other a breath away.

"Pedro is right. You are very pretty." He smiled even as Rosa slid her muddy hand across his ear and down his jawbone. He gave the muddy child a kiss. "I hope Miss Meredith can say the same for me."

Meredith adjusted the little boy in her arms and pretended to consider the notion. "I think it is a definite improvement."

"Well. Well. Well. Isn't this a charming scene?" interrupted Sonya, sounding bored as she stood with her hands on her hips. Her voice reminded Meredith of when her teachers used their fingernails on the blackboard.

CHAPTER 17

Several of the children approached Sonya, but she took a step back. Her nose wrinkled in horror as she held up both her hands to hold them at bay. "No hugs. You're filthy."

The two older children holding the water hose with the spray going full force turned back toward Axel and Meredith for just a couple of seconds. They now looked like they had just played in the mud.

Rosa wiggled down and walked up to her. "It's okay, Miss Sonya. I will make them bathe."

Instantly they turned the hose toward the movie star, missing Rosa altogether. A scream escaped Sonya's mouth, and her hands were flying in all directions like a Ninja fighting a spiderweb.

"Stop. Stop," she screamed.

One more step backward, and she slipped into the mud puddle they'd created. The water hit the puddle and bounced mud over her body and hair. The white blouse was now chocolate color, as was her skin.

"Enough, boys. Rosa, go to Meredith."

She obeyed as he walked over to Sonya and pulled her up out of the hole. He couldn't help but burst into laughter at the once-prissy prima donna who huffed and puffed at her hair that had fallen out of the tightly twirled bun at her nape. She flung the mud at him, only to have it thrown back.

"Come on. You can clean up inside." Axel choked back his amusement.

He turned to explain to Meredith he needed to take care of this, but she was flinging mud at the children then grabbed the hose and chased them around the yard. She was yelling idle threats at them for getting her muddy, and laughing. He wondered if he had ever heard anything so beautiful. Glancing back at Sonya who was trying desperately to remove mud from her clothes and body only made him understand how he had dodged a bullet when he left Hollywood.

Now, what was he going to do about Meredith?

When Meredith had hosed herself off enough to step inside and be handed a towel by Sister Elena, she could hear loud voices coming from somewhere in the house. After rubbing her face, she wrapped it around her shoulders.

"Someone isn't happy from the sound of it," Meredith said with as much disinterest as she could muster.

"Axel is driving her to the Belize Resort. It's about an hour away. Guess they'll get things straightened out along the way." She shrugged. "Or they won't." She concealed her mouth behind a wrinkled hand mischievously.

"I'm going to run back to the hotel and change

clothes. I'll come back for a visit, then we need to talk. The twins seem to be 100 percent the last couple of days. No worries there."

It was obvious to Meredith by the twinkle in the sister's eyes and the lack of concern about their intended talk, she was still counting on a miracle. That ship had sailed. The sooner she could leave here, the sooner they could move on with their lives. And if all went well, she would make sure their future needs would be taken care of. Besides, what else was she going to do with all that money? It wasn't like she'd earned it.

~ ~ ~ ~

Nathan chewed his bottom lip. Why hadn't she told him about the money? Nathan's lawyer informed him that he was the major suspect in his ex-wife's disappearance. Being charged with murder was not part of his big plan. He wanted to patch things up with her. Meredith had stood by him until the very end, paying off his debt to those rock trolls who threatened to kill him. She'd used her inheritance to help him out. But what about the rest of the money? Where was it? He needed it to start over.

Where did she go? The Russians taunted him with the news they privately had helped her. Making it appear he murdered her meant he'd go to jail and be tortured the rest of his life. Just because his debt was paid didn't mean they forgave him. With the help of a private detective his law firm employed, he discovered she'd been planning a change for some time. He traveled to a small town where he discovered she'd opened a new checking and savings account.

"I'm sorry, Mr. Marshall, but unless your name is on it, we can't give you any information on your wife's account." He never bothered to tell them Marshall was Meredith's maiden name. His surname was Andrews. Besides, this was coming from a clerk. What did a clerk know anyway? He knew it was against policy even as she walked away. As luck would have it, he ran into the president of the bank and introduced himself.

"So, you're the lucky fella," he said, inviting him into his office.

"Lucky?"

The president winked and held his finger up to his lips. "Yes. I've been expecting you, well Meredith, actually. But your name isn't on the account, so I can't give you access to your wife's safety deposit box."

"Seriously? I could have sworn she came in a few weeks ago."

The president checked his calendar on the computer and sobered. "Oh." That spoke volumes. "I'm very sorry, Mr. Marshall, or whoever you are. There's nothing I can do at this time." He stood nervously and fanned his hand out toward the door. "You'll need to bring Mrs. Marshall in with you next time or..." His voice faded, but the intent was clear. The bank president would call the police. Apparently, the man knew his wife was missing, and, according to last night's news, he was the biggest suspect.

Now, here he was, spending the night in his dinky apartment watching Entertainment Weekly when he caught a break.

~ ~ ~ ~

The Belize Barrier Resort was crawling with activity and not the kind he liked. It was paparazzi, entertainment TV, and nosey bystanders. They appeared to be waiting for something. When Sonya flipped down the mirror to check her makeup in the truck he borrowed, he realized she'd made some calls to stage a grand entrance. This was when it came in handy to know a few people from your past.

He pulled off the side of the road and texted an old friend and waited for a response. It only took a second to be guided to a safe, unobserved area where he could slip in unnoticed.

"Who were you texting? Another one of your girlfriends?" she snipped hatefully.

"Can't have you making another scene with your jealous cat routine, Sonya." He smirked. "You don't do well with competition."

"I hate you," she huffed and folded her arms across her chest.

"No, you don't. You're mad because you think I cheated on you. Meredith is a friend. She's good to the children and to Sister Elena, who, by the way, is my family. Remember?"

"I wanted to be your family," she sniffed.

"You have no idea what family means, Sonya. Let's just end this, here and now. We are bad for each other, and you know it." He pulled into the back entrance where his friend waited. "I'll see you inside then I'm gone. Live your life. That's what I intend to do."

~ ~ ~ ~

The weather had brightened later in the day after a few downpours. But the forecast was still ominous with the storm being named. People were still being warned to avoid swimming, and boating excursions had been canceled. Flights were expected to stop the following day. The puddle-jumper airlines were encouraging people to take an earlier flight if they planned to leave.

Meredith sat on the porch swing listening to the rustle of the palms and the splash of puddles as cars navigated the potholes filled with water in this part of town. Nearer the center of the tourist district, the water had drained and merely glistened under the streetlamps that flickered to life. Darkness fell softly with the gray clouds masking a moon that still occasionally tried to bounce free and promise better times.

The "talk" with Sister Elena had not happened as planned. By the time she'd returned, some of the other children had begun to feel poorly and, within an hour of her return, were running fevers. They had appeared fine when she left. Rosa and Pedro were more quiet and needy than usual but didn't complain. With more stripping of beds, fluids, rest, and reading books, they all appeared to be comfortable. Sister Elena said Father Dominic had requested her presence on the other side of town for a meeting with other church officials. Meredith offered to stay and help the staff manage things by keeping an eye on the children.

She heard giggling and loud whispers in one of the rooms when she decided to peek around the corner. To her surprise, several of the children held their faces to the light on the nightstand. As soon as she walked in, they collapsed on their beds, looking like death warmed over. She felt the forehead of a boy named Edwardo.

"I do believe you will not live to morning with this fever. I'm sorry," she confessed.

"No. No. Miss Meredith, I will live. Don't be sad. We played a trick on you. None of us are sick." He reached out and pulled her down next to him. Pedro crawled into her lap.

"We just don't want you to go. Sister Elena said—"

Another child poked him to stop talking.

"Ah. Sister Elena will be going to confession soon, I think." She ruffled his black hair. "I'm glad you are not sick."

Instead of being irritated, part of her felt relief on the delay of the talk. Sister Elena returned for dinner then the process of baths, stories, and being tucked into bed began. The woman was exhausted and frustrated.

"Can you believe they want to close us down?" she huffed. "Father Dominic thinks these children should be placed in foster care. Says we don't have enough funds to last two more months." She shook her head. "We need a miracle. Can you stay a little longer tonight? I'm going to my room and pray."

Meredith hugged her and promised to stay until the night shift arrived.

"Oh. You wanted to talk to me about something."

"It can wait, Sister. A miracle is more important."

Now here she sat, listening to children sing from somewhere in the house they called home, and listening to the occasional ping of dripping rain that trickled from downspouts to a metal bucket. The porch was protection from the humid breeze that carried wet droplets from the bushes ladened with flowers.

A figure caught her eye as he moved off the boardwalk and navigated the traffic before he crossed the street toward the orphanage. Axel. He, too, had had a long day. Would he still want to talk? There seemed to be a lot of that going on around here. Had he reconciled with the starlet by their makeup routine? For some reason, she tried to block the image out of her brain.

He took the steps two at a time and stopped when the dappled light from the window spilled onto the swing. "Can I join you?"

She patted the spot next to her and hoped he didn't take the gesture as a more personal invitation. "If you're looking for Sister Elena, I'm afraid she's turned in for the evening. I'm waiting for the night volunteers. I wouldn't be surprised if I end up staying the night."

She told him what the children had done to keep her from leaving. His grin gave her goose bumps she didn't want to feel. So, she switched topics and told him about Father Dominic's plans.

"Maybe this will help." He dug in his pants pocket and pulled out an engagement ring with the biggest diamond Meredith had ever seen.

"Holy cow. Sorry. No pun intended."

"I told Sonya it was over—again—and I wanted her to get on with her life without me. Of course, she was already doing that but didn't want to be the one rejected." He twisted the ring around to catch the light. "I told her to keep the ring, but she suggested I put it where the sun doesn't shine. Fortunately, I caught it midflight." He exhaled like he'd been running a marathon. "Just finished paying it off, too. Fifty grand."

Meredith whistled as she leaned in to get a better look.

"I checked on the way back. I think I can get about forty for it from people I know in Belize City. That should help with expenses for the next few months until I get paid."

"Sister Elena's miracle." She tilted her head to see him better in a new light and interest. Had she got it all wrong?

CHAPTER 18

Together, Meredith and Axel made a final check on the children of the orphanage as the night team made their beds and settled in for the evening. They knew to be quiet and had brought books to read until they were ready to turn out the lights. Luis had left the night shift some sweet treats and a note to tell them to stick around for breakfast.

"He's like that," Axel explained as they drove up in front of her hotel. "About twice a week, he fixes a big breakfast and thinks by feeding them, they won't quit. So far, so good. I think he uses his own money on those days to feed the extra mouths."

"A good man," she said, opening the door. "As are you, I'm thinking."

He put the Jeep into park and his hand on the back of her seat. "You weren't so sure about that last night."

"Things went a little fast on the beach and I"—she turned her focus on his blue eyes— "I guess the Caribbean atmosphere knocked my guard down. It's been a while since I let anyone get that close and realized what I had missed. That put you in a really awkward position with Sonya. I never meant to embarrass you or make things worse between you."

His silence unnerved her as he studied her intently and toyed with her hair. She swung the door open quickly and hopped out. "Thanks for bringing me back."

She closed the door. As she started up the steps, she turned to see him pull into a parking spot. Even though she quickened her escape, Axel caught up with her. Before she could respond, he took her hand and pulled her inside. The security guard spotted him and approached.

"Now, Axel. No funny stuff tonight." His eyes went to Meredith who displayed a blush. "Are you okay, miss?"

Meredith released Axel's hand and gave a nervous reply. "Yes. Thank you. For everything," she said as she glanced at Axel.

"She means me, I think. I promise I'll be a good boy. I'm just going to talk to the lady, which I tried to do last night, but that bronzed midlife-crisis playboy tried to impress the ladies."

"Okay. But I'll be over there in that big chair with a cold one in my hand. Call if you need me, miss."

"Do you know everyone in town?" Meredith asked as they found a rattan love seat among some palms near a picture window.

"Well, just in this part of town. The fancy new stuff out by the airport, I avoid. Tourists are loud, ask too many questions, and get in the way. This is better for me. And rarely am I recognized by some off-the-grid wannabe."

"So, you're a big TV star. That show was very popular. It must have been disappointing when they canceled it."

He laughed. "I quit. They threw more money at me, so I went two more seasons and then I couldn't do it anymore. There was also Sonya to deal with, which I couldn't do, either. It was easier to run away and try to forget. My contract included syndication royalties. Lucky for me, they have been lucrative. I also wrote a couple of books while I was doing the show, and they continue to do well." He shrugged. "I like things simple. Anyway, we were going to talk today before we became human mudpies." He chuckled, causing Meredith to do the same. "You took that pretty well."

"Made me feel like a kid again. I knew I'd be leaving, probably tomorrow if I can get a flight, and wanted to do something the children might remember me by."

Axel frowned and leaned farther back on the love seat. "Tomorrow? Last flight is in the morning. Not even that if the storm turns this way."

"I planned to leave today after telling Sister Elena, but she kept avoiding me. Guess I should have left when I could. I thought I needed one more day anyway. Leaving Pedro and Rosa breaks my heart."

"You're running away, too."

"Yes." She focused on her hands. "It's for the best."

"For who? You?" he asked with little emotion.

"You're the one who wanted me to leave in the first place," she said in bewilderment.

"Are you running from the ex-husband or something else?"

"What else would there be?"

"Maybe the Russian mob, stolen money, a plan to make your husband look like he murdered you—"

"What are you taking about?" she asked hotly. "Never mind. I don't even want to know." She pushed off the love seat. "This is just more of I'm so much better than you rhetoric. You're a piece of work, you know that?"

Axel got to his feet, too, and stepped closer only to have her retreat. "No. That wasn't my intent. Those two with you last night aren't who you think they are. I just wondered if maybe they were following you. I think you're in danger, Meredith."

"What about the Flynns—the married couple?" With her temper rising, she crossed her arms across her chest, a defensive move.

"Not Flynn. One of them goes by the name Jonas. Do you know where they are now? Have you seen them all day?"

"Well no. I've been busy. I tried to call them once to see how things were going, but the front desk said they had left. I thought maybe they went out to breakfast. I haven't had time to check back. Maybe I should do that now." The rhythm of her voice had slowed as she glanced over at the front desk as if they would magically appear.

"No. They checked out early this morning. After you bailed me out, I'm guessing. My buddy over there, the one who looks like a rock troll? He followed them. Headed to the airport."

"So, they're gone. Big deal. You hurt him. Maybe he decided to go home to get his doctor to check him out."

"The airport closed two hours ago. I had to detour because of some flooding. That's why I was late. The roads will get worse if that storm doesn't turn soon. The wind may get worse as well, which makes a rain feel like needles when it hits going horizontal. Even if the storm stays out to sea, they'll have no place to go. Trust me, they haven't gone far."

"They could have flown out this morning."

"Everything was completely booked. They're still here, and I'd really like to know why they came in the first place. They were definitely following you. The guy said as much last night."

"What about that other stuff you said?"

"I have a buddy who checked them out—"

"And me?" she fumed.

"Yes. But—"

"You spied on me? Am I that suspicious or dangerous?" She turned to walk away, but he cut off her retreat.

"Just let me finish," he insisted. He noticed the bruiser of a security guard stand up. He didn't want that guy punching him a second time. Lowering his voice, he continued. "Whatever you did, I don't care. Whatever you're hiding. I still don't care."

She shoved past him and stormed toward the hall that led to her room. He held up a hand to security and then shrugged. "Women," he mouthed and grinned. The security guard sat back down and picked up his magazine.

By the time Meredith retrieved her door key, Axel was on her heels. Just as the door flew open, she spun around, causing him to crash into her. The momentum pushed them into the room. In a split second, he used his foot to shut the door and pulled her into his arms. He could feel her tense and saw the fear in her eyes.

"I'm going to scream—" she started to say, but he lowered his mouth to hers and kissed her passionately, trying not to hurt her. When she began to relax, he continued to hold her but left his lips a breath away.

"Don't be afraid, Meredith. I would never hurt someone with so much love in them for those kids. You have made such a difference in this place in the short time you've been here. Yes, I wanted you gone and yes, I had you investigated. That's because they are the only family I have, and I've seen a lot of well-meaning do-gooders come and go, only to break their hearts. You appear out of nowhere, and Sister Elena tells me it was a miracle you came. You know by now what an optimist she is. Someone has to look after her and the children."

A tear slid down from the corner of her eye. Her hands were against his chest. For whatever reason, she wouldn't make eye contact. "I-I have done things. It's better that I leave." She pushed away.

"I'm afraid it's too late to leave. For once, I'm actually glad the hurricane is out there. At least now I'll have a little more time to make amends for all the pain I've caused you."

"I don't understand what you said you found out. How?"

"I have a friend who does intelligence work for some government agencies. He's the best. Army buddy. Spent some time down here with me. Has a soft spot for Sister Elena."

She moved another step away. "What do you think you know?"

"You're somehow involved with the Russian mob, for one thing." He reached for her hand, but she jerked free. "Just tell me what you're involved in. Maybe I can help."

"No one can help me. You don't need to worry."

"Well, it's not all about you," he growled. "Bad publicity could be bad for the orphanage. The diocese is looking for a way to shut it down."

"I'll take care of them. I've got money. I just can't get to it right now."

"Where did it come from?"

She glared at him.

"I want to know right now, or I'm calling the police and all those paparazzi back at the resort."

"No," she said in panic. "You can't do that. Nathan will find me."

"Well, your Russian friends took care of that. They left so much evidence that he'd killed you that now he's either already in jail or on the run. Maybe he's even dead."

"It was supposed to look like a kidnapping or that I had an accident and just walked away from it all. And, trust me, there was plenty to make me want to do that. Anyone who knew me would have been able to tell the authorities I talked about walking away from everything. Yuri promised nothing would happen to Nathan, especially since I paid off his debt. They helped me get away." She confessed how she had made last-minute plans to come to Belize when she saw Sister Elena in the airport. "I remembered her offer. When she saw me, she was so happy. I knew I had a safe place to go."

Axel huffed and paced. "And the money? My buddy says you opened another bank account in another town."

"It's a lot of money."

"Did you steal it from the Russians?" he growled.

"No. It's good money. I just can't collect it right now. But I promise I'll take care of the children. I need a little more time."

"Where. Did. It. Come. From?" he said slowly to manage his rising anger. How could she put them all in danger?

"Why does that even matter? It's my money. It's in a safe place and—"

He pivoted away from her and pulled out his phone.

"What are you doing?" she said, running around to face him. "Stop. Stop," she begged. He laid the cell phone against his chest. "Stop," she whispered. "I'll tell you everything. Please."

CHAPTER 19

Nathan arrived in Belize City on a wing and a prayer. His credit card, like his life, was nearly maxed out again. With cash in hand, he found his way to the Belize Barrier Resort where the famous Sonya Lavenworth had given her interview to one of those entertainment TV shows. Hinting at a follow-up report gave him hope he could intercept her to find out about Meredith and where she was staying.

The resort was his cup of tea: luxurious and expensive. And if he played his cards right, he'd be able to afford it after discovering Meredith's nasty and unexpected secret. How could she have betrayed him like that? Where was the generous and easy-to-manipulate woman he'd married? Was it the loss of control on his part, when he had hurt her one too many times, even though he'd been deeply sorry? Hadn't she forgiven him—again? Well, he wanted his share of the money, and he'd do whatever it took to get it.

Unfortunately, Yuri and Anton were waiting at the airport for him. They were always two steps ahead of his plans. He continued to pretend to be the gullible lawyer with a gambling problem, in hopes of staying alive. After he told them what was underway, they agreed to help him for a share of the money. In spite of not finding a body, he knew the authorities were about to arrest him for the murder of his wife. The Russians said they'd take care of everything. No worries.

And here he was.

It was early when he spotted a few of the television crews he'd watched on TV. They were drinking coffee as if they needed it attached like an intravenous drip. No doubt the bar had been busy after a once-in-a-lifetime interview with the beautiful Sonya Lavenworth.

A short note about who he was and his connection to the star was delivered by a pretty waitress after he slipped her a one-hundred-dollar bill. He was standing on the terrace, hoping for a reaction to the note, when the reporter surveyed the area then spotted him. Taking one more sip of coffee, the man rose from the table and apparently said something funny, causing the others to make some kind of joke in return. He slowly walked out onto the terrace and passed him. Nathan felt shock at being snubbed until the reporter lifted his chin in a direction for him to follow.

~ ~ ~ ~

The news the following morning wasn't good concerning the tropical storm. Although it didn't appear it would make a direct hit, it would come close enough to cause flooding and possible wind damage. There was a strong expectation for the storm to be upgraded to a hurricane by evening. Meredith packed her things after spilling the truth to Axel concerning the entire events of the last month. There were tears of regret at endangering this new place she loved, joyfulness at having escaped the abuse, and anxiousness at what to do next.

Through it all, he had listened, standing nonchalant like this was no big deal. His face remained solemn, and he spoke in a nonjudgmental tone. His cool, collected appearance reminded Meredith of a superhero. When she finished telling him about the money, he let out a whistle.

"A lottery winner."

"The biggest winner ever."

"I think I heard about that. Close to a billion? No wonder you escaped with the clothes on your back. Money like that can bring you more problems than it's worth." He stepped up next to her slowly, as if he thought she'd jump out of her skin. The truth was, she loved his nearness, his rock-solid strength. "First off, you've been here too long. I don't trust that they don't know about the money. And I don't know who Mr. and Mrs. Perfect—"

"The Flynns."

"Right. I don't know who they are. They don't have a footprint my friend can find. That in itself speaks volumes. Besides being pretenders, they were clearly following you. Mr. Flynn practically admitted he was more than just a honeymooner."

He went on to tell her about the confrontation, how he'd broke into their room, and that Flynn admitted there was a hidden camera. Finally, he told her to pack a bag. They were leaving, to be on the safe side. He excused himself to talk to the desk clerk. When he returned, Meredith decided to admit to finding the gun and her picture in the pocket of a jacket.

"I thought he was rich and carried a gun for protection. I don't know, at the time it made sense. The picture of me… I later rationalized that it was dark in there. Thought maybe I was jazzed on adrenaline and made a mistake. I was more concerned at checking him over and reassuring his wife—well, pretend wife. In the end, I went to my room and tried to rest. I got up early and headed to the beach. I wanted to decide on the best way to tell Sister Elena I planned to leave."

"But you didn't."

"No. I ran into your fiancée, and I'll have to say, your taste in women leaves a lot to be desired," she said, rolling her eyes.

Axel rubbed the side of his beard. "I'm no catch according to her agent, press secretary, and the gossip rags. I'm too crude, rough, and off the grid, both mentally and physically." His grin was infectious. "Do I want to know what she had to say?"

"Not unless you want me to stutter and blush retelling how the two of you solved your disagreements." She laughed so hard she flopped on the bed, placing her hand on her heart. "I didn't hang around to chat very long. Lost my appetite. When I got to the orphanage, Sister Elena avoided me with her list of chores, even though I followed like an obedient puppy."

"All packed?" he asked patiently as she nodded. "We'll find another place. I checked at the desk when you started packing and the Flynns checked out early and in a hurry. No idea where they went. The clerk did verify that they showed an interest in your whereabouts almost daily. Not sure if they were to friend or protect you."

"I find it odd they left without checking on me or leaving a way to contact them."

Axel grabbed her backpack and slung it over his shoulder in order to carry her suitcase. "I agree. All the more reason to find a new place. They may expect you to stay put since the storm is intensifying and may think you're on the outs with me."

"Where are we going?"

"If the seas weren't so rough, I'd take you to my boat. But I had it moved while I was gone, to a safer place where the waves wouldn't bash it to pieces. I have another place. Too late and too dark to go tonight. I called Juan. He's going to put us up for the night."

"Us?" she said wide-eyed. "I'm not endangering anyone else because of my bad decisions. Juan has a family. I'll stay here."

Axel dropped the bags. "Fine. Me, too. I'm not letting you out of my sight." He placed his hands on his waist like a drill sergeant and waited. "You have the room for another night." He went to the French doors, checked the locks then drew the drapes. "I'll let Juan know and we can go to bed."

"Excuse me?" she gasped.

"I'll take the couch. Makes into a bed." She continued to stare at him. He kicked off his sandals then grabbed a pillow off her bed. "I snore. Do you?"

"No. It's just..." She blushed and hugged her arms.

"I make you nervous." The corner of his mouth formed a straight hard line. "Last night. Us. I liked it. I thought you did, too." She remained silent and lowered her eyes, until he came over and lifted her chin with one finger. "I'm here to make sure things don't go sideways. I don't know where the Flynns are and—"

"Axel," she whispered. Realizing he was a breath away caused her to shred the last ounce of doubt she had about him. He was nothing like she feared and everything missing in her life. "I." Before she could confess her feelings, he pulled her into his arms and they melted into the love their lives had yearned for in a world of impossible roadblocks and missteps.

"We can do this together. Please. Just let me in."

Meredith rested her head against his shoulder as his arms tightened around her. "I'm afraid if I don't leave, I'll hurt the work Sister Elena is doing."

A light knock caused Axel to rush to the door. He jerked it open to see the hotel muscle.

"You better turn on the TV, Axel. Your crazy girlfriend has a lot to say about you."

~ ~ ~ ~

Axel recognized the elegant lobby of the Belize Barrier Resort. The number of paparazzi stood packed in a semicircle as if waiting for something or someone.

"This was taped earlier. Time stamp is midafternoon," the security guard said as he pointed the remote toward the TV to increase the volume.

Axel relaxed his arms at his side and waited for the bombshell he knew was coming. Cameras clicked and flashed as the star strolled out, appearing stricken but beautiful, her assistant waiting as if to lift a royal train if needed. Sonya was dressed in a sundress that probably cost more than Sister Elena's operating expenses for a month. The sun hat, meant to cover her identity along with the sunglasses, merely marked her as the person of interest they were waiting for.

He was very aware of the role of her assistant who had been close by when they arrived earlier. Most likely the crowd of reporters and paparazzo had been summoned by her. She was the kind of person who would enjoy tossing bloody meat in a pool of piranha.

Cameras clicked as she paused and listened to something her assistant said in her ear. He'd seen it before; she walked in with her head in the clouds and her assistant gave her information which caused her to focus on the moment. The scripted encounters had amused him when he first met her then it got to be every time they went to a restaurant, weekend trip, or stroll on the beach. The woman loved attention. Their biggest arguments were when they'd been alone, away from the limelight and lots of people. In public, they were the ideal Hollywood lovebirds.

Sonya motioned for the Entertainment Weekly TV reporter to approach and took him aside while cameras continued to click. In a few minutes, she disappeared, and the reporter faced the cameras.

"Movie great, Sonya Lavenworth has revealed she and her long-time fiancé, Axel Cahill, have split. She gave no indication as to the reason for the relationship failure but suggested Axel had problems they couldn't work through. She concluded by saying she hopes he is able to resolve some issues he suffers from and gets the help he needs."

Axel remained stoic and unaffected by her words. He stared at the television even after the security guard turned it off.

"You got issues I don't know about, Axel?" the guard asked.

Finally, he turned his head toward the guard and exhaled. "Yeah. We need a safe place to go. If I know Sonya, she is going to tell all in a few hours and dump all over Meredith. People are searching for her, and not the friendly kind. Can you help?"

"You wanna go, miss?" he asked Meredith.

"Yes."

"Did you break the law?"

She swallowed hard. "I'm not sure. But if my ex-husband finds me, then I'm not going to be able to help Sister Elena or work at the clinic."

His bottom lip protruded as he nodded. "Come with me."

CHAPTER 20

The assistant handed Sonya a scribbled note the entertainment reporter had delivered. They had a good relationship, and she often counted on him to expose her in the best possible light when it came to a celebrity scoop.

She read the note at the open sliding glass doors, in case anyone might be using the moment for a candid photo as the wind gusts toyed with the silk robe she wrapped around her perfect body. It caressed her down to the middle of her tanned thighs. Her hair, pulled into a ponytail, revealed a long, slender neck. There was enough of her skin showing that kept her decent, while teasing possible skillful paparazzi if they zeroed in on her room and movements.

"Bring him to me," she said to the assistant as she reread the note. "And the reporter. The one who is always so helpful. I promised him an interview this morning. Order coffee, and I'll get dressed. Tell them I'll see them in one hour." As the door shut, she walked over to the rattan-framed mirror hanging next to the door and admired herself, turning her head this way and that. "Now, what should we do about Meredith Marshall?"

~ ~ ~ ~

The hotel security guard took Axel and Meredith to his mother's house in the jungle. It was almost thirty minutes from town. He promised to let Sister Elena know they were safe. The old lady who offered her house was eager to help and spoke a mixture of English and Mayan. In spite of no electricity due to the storm, she was cooking in a firepit under a breezeway structure between the house and a garage. She brewed coffee and had a camper-style oven on one end where she prepared some kind of pastry.

"Did you sleep well with the rain and wind howling?" she asked Axel the next morning then turned her eyes to Meredith. "She your woman?"

Before Meredith could answer, he responded in what she assumed was Mayan, one of the languages of the area. The woman grinned and winked at her then slapped Axel on the bottom, making him give her a kiss on the cheek.

No matter where he went, people liked him. He treated them with respect and kindness. This had not been the case with her when she arrived. Now, although it felt like he was treading lightly around her, the attraction between them felt real. But, then again, how would she even know what real felt like? At least, for her, his nearness, the sound of his voice, and the way he moved with confidence gave her a yearning she'd never experienced.

"What did you tell her about me?" She took the chipped cup of coffee he handed her and followed him into the kitchen.

"I told her we had become friends," he said, going to the window. Then he turned around. "She assumed we slept together last night since we were in the same room."

"Oh. And you do snore," she accused. The way he stared at her, as if memorizing her face, caused an uneasiness to spring up inside her.

"Didn't seem like the right time to—share my interest." He drained his cup of coffee and set it down on the counter. "Besides, twin beds aren't my idea of a good place for romance."

She focused on the inside of her empty cup, not knowing how to respond. Did she want romance, a warm body of reassurance, or a deep abiding love? Was there even such a thing anymore?

"Hey"—he took the cup from her hands—"I think we can both agree we've made peace."

She nodded acceptance and dared meet his gaze.

"I'm not sure what to think about you or all of this, but I do believe you did the right thing running away. However, that is going to have to be straightened out." He slid his hand from the top of her shoulder down her arm until he took her hand. "I'm sorry for the way I treated you at first. I misjudged you."

The security guard who had brought them to safety walked in and tossed Axel keys. "My SUV should get you there. Road is still clear for now. I think maybe a couple of hours and the storm is going to hit us. Just a glancing blow, but we'll still have flooding. You can get to your place in plenty of time now that the sun is up."

"Where are we going? I thought we were staying here?" Meredith asked.

"I have a place between the mountains and the coast. We'll be safer there," Axel was quick to say.

"What about the hurricane? The children?"

"They have been moved inland and are safe. Luis and his sister saw to that. Several others in town came to help." Axel shook his friend's hand then turned to Meredith. "We need to go. Now."

"Axel." The security guard leaned in closer. "There are a few extra necessities I packed for you. Know what I mean?"

"You're a good man, Hector."

Hector tilted his head toward the door. "Via con Dios, my friend." Go with God.

"You as well."

~ ~ ~ ~

Most of the road was a mixture of gravel and potholes, slowing the SUV down at times. One place had water starting to run over the surface but was clear enough to know there were no missing sections to send them down the side of the mountain. For short periods of time, it felt like the storm had abated when they passed between rocky walls that had been blasted out to create the road. It led to some mountain villages and, on the east side, was Guatemala.

Axel hoped this storm didn't hit them but moved north into Mexico or even farther into Texas. Those people didn't need any more problems to add to their poverty. From the reports, they would not get the full impact. His place along the coast, and surrounded by mountains, would be a good safe place to be if the Flynns continued to search for Meredith.

The storm intensified more quickly than expected, making the one-hour drive almost three. There were times the windshield wipers couldn't keep up with the heavy rain. Stopping the car was out of the question in case of landslides or getting stuck in the mud. Neither of them spoke much, and he chose to concentrate on the road ahead of them. Several times, a sudden burst of wind rocked the vehicle, but the four-wheel drive enabled them to keep going.

When he neared his place, he found a safe spot to pull over and check his phone. He had a message from Hector again. "Your movie star girlfriend had an interview this afternoon. It was on the news. I'll send you a link. Miss Meredith is wanted for questioning. Did you know that?" Then a link appeared.

"What is it?" she asked as he connected to the link and held it for both of them to watch.

It appeared to be from an afternoon news show in the States. The host reported on the hurricane in Central America then let the weatherman explain where it was headed in relationship to the United States. For now, that was where it was headed. The report lasted a full thirty seconds then the host added a celebrity alert, which they did every day.

"Actress Sonya Lavenworth was spotted in the hurricane-prone country of Belize yesterday. Rumors have been flying that she and longtime partner and fiancé Axel Cahill were headed for trouble. They haven't been spotted together for several months."

"I haven't been a longtime partner in about eighteen

months," he grumbled.

He glanced at Meredith to gauge her reaction, but her attention to the report suggested she might be listening from a standpoint of curiosity. Nothing more. Why he wanted her to know he and Sonya hadn't been an item for a long time baffled him.

The truth still remained: she was going to leave sooner rather than later, and, with the kind of money she was hiding, she could well afford to escape to a remote island in the Hebrides. Like many out-of-the-way places, a medical staff was always welcome, and they would do whatever necessary to keep her safe and happy. With his name recognition, that probably wasn't going to be possible now.

The report continued.

"We now take you to our entertainment affiliate and reporter Jordon Chevelle. Jordon, there's been a lot of speculation about these two over the last couple of years, especially since Axel left his very popular show, Celebrity Outback."

"Yes, there sure has. I have two clips for you. This first one is last night when Sonya was spotted at the Barrier Resort." The take was less than a minute, but she was gracious and patient with the reporters. "So, if you couldn't hear all that, Sonya said she'd come down to meet with Axel Cahill, her on-again off-again romance. Said that she discovered some disturbing information and had broken off the engagement."

Meredith hit the pause bars and shifted her attention to him. "Disturbing information? What is she talking about?"

"Her eyelash technician canceled her next appointment for all I know."

Meredith unpaused the bars to continue the film.

The reporter stood in the lobby and scrolled through his tablet as if checking information that might preclude World War III. The camera panned out as he continued. "I sat down with Sonya this morning in her suite over coffee to have an informal conversation about where she goes from here. The woman is tougher than she appears as you'll find out tonight on the Entertainment Weekly TV exclusive. You won't want to miss it."

"There!" Meredith said as the segment went back to the main host. "Scroll back. No, that's too far." Axel adjusted the film. She pointed at the screen and it stopped it again. "Can you make it bigger? I want to see the men standing to the side. Almost out of camera range." She jerked back in her seat as if she'd been shot.

"Who is it?"

She stared wide-eyed out the windshield being pelted with rain.

"Meredith?"

"The one in the middle is my ex-husband, Nathan. The men on either side of him are the Russians who helped me escape." She slowly turned to face Axel, tears pooling in the corners of her eyes. "By now they know where I am, thanks to Sonya Lavenworth."

CHAPTER 21

Axel proceeded toward his home away from home, hoping the area where he built his compound would be protected from the worst of the wind. The road turned muddy as the rain increased. The SUV swerved several times when the mud became slippery and thick. A waterfall that usually spilled over the cliff and down in a rocky creek shot farther out, hitting the road with muddy spray. He gunned the vehicle, ramming through, not knowing if the road remained on the other side.

Other than a few potholes, they dodged a bullet as to the road being washed out. Stealing a glance to the rearview mirror, he could see the water was now shooting over the road completely, forming an arch over where they had just passed. That should keep the road in better condition. It would also allow unwanted guests the ability to follow.

"Where are we going, Axel?" Meredith asked as she continued to grip the seat with one hand and the other on the dash. "Can you even see out the windshield?"

The rain felt like it was dumping water on them with buckets and now only his wiper worked, leaving her blind to what lay ahead, which might be for the best.

"Headed to my place. Almost there. I can see just fine…" He paused when his wiper stuck. He applied the brakes slowly, but the back end still fishtailed. It took muscle to keep it from going over what he knew to be a cliff. He powered the window down and reached out to grab the wiper, popped it several times before it started its sluggish back-and-forth.

Pulling his soaked arms back inside, he spotted a few boulders ahead sliding down the hillside toward the ocean. Knowing the signs of a mudslide waiting to happen, he didn't waste time to power up the window. He remembered this SUV had a powerful engine and a reputation for being a perfect all-terrain vehicle, he propelled forward toward the area that could either kill them or block an enemy. He shifted into four-wheel drive as Meredith sucked in her breath.

"We're not going to make it," she yelled as trees fell on her side of the car.

"Just watch me," he shouted above the grind of the car and lightning striking behind them.

The road widened enough for two cars, but debris forced him to swerve several times, throwing Meredith's shoulder into his. He glanced at her for a split second and saw silent tears cascading down her cheek as she bit her bottom lip, but she remained silent, focusing ahead with terror-filled eyes.

The movement of earth beneath them alerted Axel the hillside was about to come down on top of them. Gunning the car, it lurched forward as if it had been given free rein. The ground appeared to melt to his left as he dodged a table-size boulder bouncing onto the road. He navigated past it by jerking the wheel right to go behind it, only to find the right side of the car had to go up. This left him steering out of a precarious tilted position that could flip them completely over, exposing them to the landslide now in motion.

A scream escaped Meredith as she covered her head against a rock that slammed into her window, causing it to spiderweb in all directions. In a split second, he had righted the vehicle back onto all four tires and sped forward while the hillside crashed and melted toward them. Crashing trees ripped from their shallow root systems rolled downward. One hit a ledge and propelled over the top of the car, barely missing them. Instinctively, they ducked, but Axel kept the car speeding ahead while the ground fell away behind them, widening as if determined to chase the two into the ocean below.

"Faster," she cried out as she turned to observe their death sentence clawing its way toward them.

The road spiraled down to where Axel's compound was, forcing him to slow down enough to take several curves. Just when he was convinced they'd outrun the slide, the wind tossed an uprooted palm across the road. There was no avoiding it this time, and he crashed into it, sending them airborne.

The car's back tires landed on the trunk of the tree. No amount of gunning the engine could jar it loose from its position until a wind gust rocked them enough to break free. Both looked at each other and gave a nervous chuckle as if they'd cheated death one more time.

However, the storm wasn't finished with them as he

tried to center the car on the road. It had become impossible to go farther without fighting the wind when they were slammed into the side of the culvert lined with rocks.

"Now what?" she asked, trying to pry open the door to no avail.

"See that black spot ahead?"

She nodded after squinting past the rain pelting the windshield.

"That's a cave. Several passages can lead us to a safer place. We've just got to get there."

"Can't we stay here?" she pleaded.

"That hillside looks iffy and I don't want to be part of another landslide." He pulled up radar on his phone. "We're almost in the eye of the storm. That will be our chance to run for it. In this wind, we'd never make it. This section is pretty protected, but there's still a chance the ground will get too saturated and loosen more trees, which could pin us down for days. Right now, I have a cell connection, but that, too, is hit or miss up here." He reached over and laid a hand on her arm then slid it down to her trembling hand. "We'll be okay. Promise."

She laid her free hand on top of his then squeezed. "You're so calm."

"I've been in worse scenarios. Trust me. I had to put myself in danger a number of times because some stupid celebrity didn't listen to me." He turned his attention to the sky as he powered his window down enough to see. "They all think they're bulletproof or something, I guess."

"Sounds like you earned every penny."

"Guess that was part of the problem. The money was

too good, and I stayed longer than I should have. Warped my perception of real life."

"But down here you're happy?"

He turned his attention back to her and pulled his hand free. "I haven't been happy for a long time, but at least here I was at peace. My demons had been put to rest, and I started to see things clearly." When she smiled at him, he realized this wet and beautiful creature had made him happy for the first time in many years. "Where on earth have you been my whole life?"

"Waiting," was all she said.

The sudden impact of calm, presented by the eye of the storm, took both of them by surprise. There was still a light spray of rain carried off the tranquil breeze. The sky started to clear, trying to trick them into believing the storm was over. As Meredith climbed over the console, Axel reached in and gave her a rescue hug to pull her forward over the seat and steering wheel. With her feet firmly on the ground he, too, looked upward.

"Don't let that patch of blue-gray sky make you too comfortable. Radar showed the eye of the storm has a small diameter. We might have thirty minutes to reach the cave. I'll get our backpacks." After slinging his into place on his back, he shouldered hers when she reached for it. "Better let me. Both our packs are heavy, and I don't want you falling or twisting an ankle out here. I do this kind of thing all the time. Okay?"

"Yes." She saluted. "Never let it be said I was a candidate for a difficult celebrity nurse."

Even now, he could feel the winds picking up and the air pressure changing. The cave wasn't far, but the road was slick with mud, slowing them down. Meredith was a good hiker in spite of having to take extra care as she stepped over vegetation debris and navigated through muddy ruts in the road.

"Almost there, Meredith. Are you doing okay? Do you need to take a break?"

"I'm good." She stopped and took in the view of the sea beyond the cliff where the road ran. "I'll take a breather once we're in the cave."

"You're a trouper," he said, adjusting her pack to his other shoulder. "We need to pick up the pace. Those clouds are starting to look ominous." Even before the last words came out of his mouth, he had doubled his speed. His long strides caused her to stretch out hers, making her appear awkward and a bit clumsy. But through it all she never complained. She was turning out to be too good to be true.

They paused for a couple of seconds, ten feet from the mouth of the cave where a rocky path led inside. The ground nearby sloped downward toward where glistening bowls of water that had eroded into the rock formations over time. Along the hillside over the mouth of the cave grew ferns, and low-growing palms mixed with tangled flowered branches yanked from the ground.

"I think the cave has taken on water, but it shouldn't be bad. There's a tunnel of water that acts like a pathway to where we want to go. Normally, it's peaceful. Might be a rough ride now."

Meredith took a deep breath then let it out slowly. She stepped sideways toward the cliff in hopes of seeing the ocean and how it may have changed during this event. "Will the ocean be calm now, too?"

"No. Even though we're in the calm part of the storm, it acts just the opposite in the ocean. The waves are still churning like it wants to kill everyone."

"Do I have time to take a look?" she said, taking another step in that direction.

"No!" he warned, raising his hand to try and grab her. But her foot hit some wet mud that acted like ice, and down she went, grabbing at the ground as her body raced toward the edge. The last thing he heard was her scream as she disappeared over the edge.

CHAPTER 22

Nathan waited an hour before the movie star, Sonya Lavenworth allowed him into the room the restaurant had set aside for her. He was both excited and intimidated she'd agreed to see him before her next interview with the reporter. The two Russians were stopped by her security, along with hotel security. Their grumpy expressions indicated extreme irritation at the matter, but he had never known them to be any other way.

The hotel manager ushered him in and warned him to be on his best behavior, that Ms. Lavenworth was an important guest and he didn't want her upset. Nathan nodded agreement as he sucked up his courage and entered. He was quickly patted down by hotel security then again by a tough guy who stood a head taller than him.

Then he saw her standing at the large windows, staring out toward the sea. Rain pelted the glass, making a snapping sound as the greenery brushed the surface like a paintbrush. The bodyguard approached her and spoke softly, causing her to turn toward him with a timid glance.

Had he ever seen such a beautiful creature? She was more stunning than her on-screen presence. Unlike many of the characters she portrayed, here she appeared fragile and frightened. But, with the grace of royalty, she offered him a thin smile. It didn't take a rocket scientist to see she was in pain. Who had done this to such an amazing woman?

"Mr. Marshall?" a woman who he imagined must be her secretary or personal assistant asked.

"Ah. No. Nathan Andrews. My wife is—"

"Follow me," she said, pivoting and walking toward the actress.

He slipped his finger in between his collar and throat, feeling the fabric tighten as he neared her. He caught his toe on a rug and stumbled into a table that held a vase of flowers. The bodyguard reached out and steadied it, leveling a disgusted frown of contempt toward him.

"Oh. Sorry," he said, looking from the bodyguard to Sonya, who was a bit taller than he expected.

"It's all right. I've found these kinds of places often like to place furniture more for the sake of show than function. Raphael, bring Mr...."

"Andrews. Nathan Andrews."

"Yes. Bring us a pot of coffee. It feels a little cool in here, I think. Come. Let's sit here to enjoy the storm."

He obeyed.

"I was expecting your name to be Marshall."

"Well, that was my wife's maiden name. When we divorced, she wanted it back."

"That must have been very painful for you," she said

softly as her head tilted innocently. "I understand that kind of pain. My fiancé has been less than honest and faithful to me. I'm brokenhearted. I guess we have more than one thing in common."

"Not only did Meredith ruin me financially, she ran off with my money to punish me for wanting to leave her."

Sonya reached out and laid her hand on his that rested on the small glass table. "I'm so sorry."

Nathan loved her light touch and regretted lying to such a fine woman. "I guess we're in the same boat," he said, laying his free hand atop hers.

"How can I help you, Nathan?" The coffee was placed on the table, the assistant quickly pouring them each a cup before moving to another part of the room. She lifted the cup and studied him over the rim.

"I saw your press conference on the TV and thought you might be able to help me find her. The reporter showed a picture of her for only a few seconds, but I recognized her immediately. She disappeared off the face of the map." He quickly told her the story how she had disappeared, leaving signs of foul play. "Now the police think I've murdered her. Ms. Lavenworth, I—"

"Please call me Sonya, dear Nathan."

"Thank you, Sonya. I need proof she is alive."

"And the money?" she cooed then took a sip of the hot brew.

"The most important thing is proving she is still alive. In spite of everything she's done to me, I wish her no harm or ill will. She touched my heart, and I hate that I wasn't enough for her, but I don't want to go to prison, either."

"And the money?" she repeated a little more

forcefully.

"If I find her, then, yes, I want the money. There is little time left that I can claim my share."

"Your share? I thought it was all your money?" she quizzed suspiciously.

"Only half. You see, Meredith Marshall was the one-billion-dollar lottery winner everyone was talking about a month ago."

"And you want to know where she is?"

He nodded.

"Then it is more than about finding your sweet love," she said with an amused tone that made Nathan cringe.

"Exactly."

"You and I have a lot in common, Nathan. I think I can help you locate the little tramp who has hoodwinked my Axel. Maybe she'll have an unfortunate accident out there in the wilds."

"That would be tragic. Maybe your Axel would be to blame."

"Oh, too bad," she smirked.

Nathan realized the sweet, angelic persona the woman before him was anything but fragile. The woman was vindictive and cunning, which had a rather pleasing effect on him. Maybe his luck was about to change.

~ ~ ~ ~

"Don't look down," he yelled. "Grab my hand. I'll pull you up!"

Meredith sobbed as she disobeyed and stole a glance down the face of the cliff to the waves crashing against the rocks below. "I can't." She clung to two protruding rocks the size of softballs, a foot apart. They were sharp and wet. Clinging to them, with her body smashed against the rugged face of the cliff, she felt shock at the way she'd caught them on her downward slide. The rain and wind intensified just as a crash of lightning caused a scream to escape from deep inside her.

"Meredith, it's now or never. Trust me."

She could see him reach down farther than he should as his body extended slightly over the edge. If she reached up, then her release of the desperate grip she held to the protruding rock would unsteady her body.

"Meredith!"

As she opened her mouth, a blast of rain slammed into her face like tiny razor blades. All she could do was nod and wiggle her fingers against the security hold. In slow motion, she eased one hand free, only to slip and grab her safety rock once more. With her head now resting against the rocky surface, she could hear his encouragement, edged with desperation.

"Remember. Take a deep breath. Visualize rocking those babies at the orphanage. They need you, Meredith. I need you. Together we can make this a better world. Trust me. Just this once."

This time, she lunged for his hand and felt it close around her wrist. With the sudden movement, her feet slipped off the ledge, and now her body dangled in the wind with nothing but his grip keeping her from a painful death on the jagged rocks below. Through the rain, she searched to see his face, barely visible, and thought she saw him grin as if amused at the situation, or was it at her foolish trust of yet another rogue.

In that moment, Meredith appreciated the fact that

this was not what she planned in the way of adventure or an escape to a different kind of life. With newfound determination, she used her free hand to catch hold of his arm. Her feet found dents in the rocks to wedge a step up, to help relieve the weight that could easily pull him over the edge. As she neared him, his grunts caught in the wind and inspired her to keep going. Forced to fight for a life unfinished, she clawed at the grass and mud on top of the cliff until she was able to release Axel's hand and crawl forward.

He had fallen backward and lay breathing hard as the rain drenched his body. Still on all fours, she reached him and fell across his chest, weeping. "Axel!" She choked and pushed back his long hair from his face. "Axel," she said more softly as he reached to pulled her down to kiss him on the side of his neck.

"We need to get out of here," he said, pushing her back and struggling to his feet. He helped her up and, together, they stumbled forward against the wind, struggling to reach the cave.

Axel picked up the backpacks he dropped then rolled his shoulders, now sore from holding onto her. They had been thrown to the side and were soaking wet. She guessed chasing after her when she took a tumble slide toward death didn't leave much time to put them in a dry or safe place. The thought that he could have easily died trying to save her made her shudder with fear. Realizing once again, she had strong feelings for this rough-and-tumble character vaporized any hesitation at following him into a cave.

The wind began its howl of destruction almost as soon as they entered. If she had not been rescued, by now the wind would have easily sent her to the rocks below. She stood watching him open his backpack and take out a couple of waterproof jackets and pants. Tossing them to her, he pulled off his outer clothes.

"We're both soaked. Won't take long for hypothermia to set in. Our bodies are under stress, especially yours. Get out of those clothes."

"But. But." Her teeth chattered as he stripped down to nothing and slipped on dry waterproof pants, shirt, and jacket. Even now, he appeared calm and determined to solve the newest problem. In spite of wanting to respond to his orders, she couldn't remove her clothing. She was trembling too hard.

In two long strides, he was at her side, pulling her shirt over her head. "It's okay, Meredith." He kept his gaze on her face as he laid the flimsy shirt on a rock. "I'll come back for your clothes when the storm is over."

Her eyelids fluttered in her nervous anticipation as he touched the waist of her shorts. "I'm going to pull these off then dress those cuts on your legs."

She opened her mouth to respond but nothing came out. Before she could resist, he was pulling them down around her ankles. His large hand went around one ankle then the other as he pulled off her muddy shoes, and finally, her shorts.

Standing in nothing but her lacy panties and bra, she followed him to his backpack where he pulled something else out. He unfolded it as he approached her again. Without warning, he pulled the new shirt over her head then wrapped the solar blanket tightly around her. He leaned back against an outcropping of rock and pulled her into his arms, rubbing her back vigorously in an up-and-down motion to the point where it almost hurt.

"I've got to get you warmed up." He then massaged her shoulders and arms. "Better?" he said, his lips nearly touching hers.

"Yes," she whispered.

"I'm going to doctor those cuts. Then I'll help you get your pants on. Hopefully we can still make it to my place. If not, we can hole up in here for a while."

As he cleaned and spread ointment on her legs, she wondered if he noticed the goose bumps. She should have been treating herself. After all, she was the medical professional. But his careful strokes ignited something inside her that was unfamiliar and pleasing.

He butterfly bandaged two areas of concern and said she could inspect his work when they were at a cleaner and drier place. Stitches were not out of the question, but she could have the final say. Kneeling at her feet, he spoke, raising his eyes to meet hers.

"I can stitch you up if needed, but I can't promise there wouldn't be a scar on these pretty legs of yours." He grinned as his hand remained on her naked limb.

When she found herself drowning in his blue eyes and silenced by his gentle attention to details, she managed to reach out and touch his face. "Thank you. I owe you, my life."

"I'm thinking maybe we'll call it even, then." He stood and retrieved the waterproof pants. Axel slipped them over her feet then pulled them up slowly, forcing her to stand up straight. He jerked the string around the waist tighter, which sent her into his body. She didn't back away, like she would have a few days earlier, and he didn't retreat. What he did do was wrap his arms around her and lower his mouth to hers. She hoped, like her, he experienced something as powerful as the raging storm that had brought them together.

"Do you always show a girl such a tumultuous time?" she said as she stole a short kiss.

"Most have expected candlelight, flowers, and an expensive dinner."

"They don't know what they're missing."

He chuckled and picked up her shoes. "I'm afraid I don't have anything better than your tennis shoes, but I do have a pair of dry socks."

"Perfect," she said, following him to where he'd placed the backpack. "Where to now?"

"You aren't going to like it."

CHAPTER 23

Meredith marveled at the amount of equipment Axel carried in his backpack. He moved like a graceful mountain goat on the rocky path that led through stalactites and stalagmites growing like a twisted white forest of calcite. He'd given her a small headlamp to wear, as did he, to see through the maze of darkness. When the beam of light reflected off the formations, a sparkle spread light for a few extra feet. Several holes in the ceiling of the cave now were funnels for rain.

Axel stopped and pointed upward. "Usually, these holes allow enough light that the small lights we're wearing aren't necessary. By the time we run out of the holes, the exit opens up to a lagoon-like area. There's plenty of light the last stretch. Only now, I'm concerned that the water is rising." He pointed toward the river. "Notice how cloudy it is? Usually, crystal clear. We've got too much coming in."

"Now what? Is there another way out of here? That current is moving pretty fast."

He pointed to a large container fastened to the rock wall. "I was hoping we'd get here before the water rose too high. It's never been like this that I know of, but you never know with a hurricane." Without warning, he started up the wall, grasping what appeared to be grab holes carved out in the rock. The image of Spiderman popped into her head as he climbed effortlessly until he reached a ledge wide enough to stand on.

The wind moaned like a disgruntled monster through the ceiling holes as the rain gushed faster, cascading below with a thunderous roar. Keeping an eye on the rising river then shifting her attention to Axel without falling into the torrents proved to be a balancing act. By the time he returned to her side, he carried a large yellow bag on his back like another backpack. There were also two metal poles laced through the straps. Handing the poles off to her, he opened the yellow contraption and it soon inflated to a small raft big enough for two. Two paddles fell to her feet, and she quickly rescued them before the lapping water snagged them. She attached them to the poles.

The raft was sturdier than she imagined, enabling Axel to stand inside it after lowering it into the water and looping the rope onto a jagged rock. After tossing the oars into the boat, he motioned for her to join him then outstretched his hand for her to take. The slippery rock ledge nearly caused her to tumble like a blow-up clown in front of a tire-and-lube store, but his strong arms caught her in time. Lowering her to a sitting position, he turned and freed their rope.

He quickly seated himself to stabilize the boat from tilting with his sudden shift of weight. In seconds, they were paddling down a river of water, trying to keep from bouncing off the rough edges of large rocks that normally were far enough away from the main stream that they were more eye candy than a danger. The current picked up speed. Axel paddled harder. She could see a tunnel of light now, that widened each second as the boat rushed closer toward the exit.

The boat swerved slightly as they emerged into a storm-tossed lake surrounded by rock formations. She noticed now Axel paddled with all he had, toward the bank, and kept glancing toward a new threat she couldn't see. When he got close enough, he stood and flung each backpack to the narrow ledge then yelled to her.

"Jump. Now!"

She tried to understand why even as he leaped to shore, slipping down on one knee then scampered up to spin toward her. The boat rocked as she tried to figure out how to jump without crashing headfirst against the rocks along the shore.

"Jump!" he yelled as he ran along the shore. He sped up against the wind and pointed toward the danger.

A monstrous waterfall rumbled and swirled downward toward an abyss she didn't want to explore. Axel ran ahead and pointed to a narrowing ledge that resembled a peninsula. Surefooted as a mountain goat, he navigated the strip of land as the raft rushed toward him.

"Jump! I got you!"

When the raft slammed into the peninsula, she leaped into his waiting arms with one foot snagging on a branch she managed to shake off. He held tight as she peered around him at the ravenous waterfall that would have killed her. The wind was stronger here. Axel led her back toward the safety of the shore where they edged along the rock wall until he reached the packs and slipped his easily onto his back. This time, he adjusted hers so she would be able to carry it.

Although the rain was blinding her, he didn't appear to struggle while leading them to safety. When he pushed back tangled vines to reveal yet another cave, she realized they had been climbing steadily upward. Now she could see the pool below and the waterfall that nearly took them to a watery grave. Once inside, he got to work.

"What are you doing?" she asked as he started pulling things out of nooks and crannies of the rock formation.

"Build us a fire." He stacked wood from some kind of protective covering near the mouth of their new refuge. "We can't go any farther until the storm passes and the sun returns. The water needs to run down first. It will as soon as the rain stops. This place looks totally different without Mother Nature having a meltdown."

"Can I help?"

"There's some dry kindling in my stash. We need it for the fire. I've also got some beef jerky and coffee in there. Hope you like instant."

"Sounds like a five-star restaurant to me."

Axel stood up to his full height and eyed her cautiously then grinned as if he were sending her a message of approval. She guessed even now they both retained some trust issues in spite of awakening feelings neither of them had experienced in some time, if ever. The thought that she continued to surprise him matched her growing hero worship of a man who showed no fear.

~ ~ ~ ~

Sister Elena helped Luis and his sister tuck the children in for the night. They had taken refuge on higher ground, along with others too afraid to stay close to the ocean. The storm surge could be a killer, although the storm wasn't the worst that had ever hit this part of Belize. The worst was over, but the rain continued and probably would taper off during the night. But flooding could be a real problem if you didn't know what kind of damage to expect when returning home. The children thought it an adventure and enjoyed being read to, having unexpected snacks, and playing card games with the older ones.

"Sister Elena." It was Luis holding out a phone to her. "Your American friend. The one who used to come down and help Axel."

She took the phone gingerly and mouthed thank you to him.

"Hello. Jake Thorn, is that you?"

"Yes, Sister Elena. Are you guys safe?"

She chuckled. "Yes. Yes. Thank you for checking on us."

"Sister, I'm worried about Axel. I've been trying to reach him. Is he with you?"

"No, he is not. He took our new friend to his place. Why?"

"Meredith Marshall?"

"Of course. Lovely girl. I think she is just what we prayed for."

"I doubt that," he said flippantly.

"What do you mean? Is something wrong?"

"You might say that. Her ex-husband is in Belize."

"Yes. We expected as much. That is why Axel is hiding her."

"And that couple who were on the plane with you? The May-December lovebirds? Well, guess what?"

"No worries. They have left town. I know. I know. The gentleman and Axel had a bit of a misunderstanding, but it all worked out. They were just trying to console Meredith and felt a little overprotective. Nothing more. They didn't even press charges, you know. I thought I was going to have to post bail, and Axel got out of jail the next morning."

"That's because Meredith bailed him out. She was afraid you'd have to use money from the orphanage fund."

"Good heavens," she sighed.

"That couple works for the US government and have been tracking Meredith for over a month. They did not fly out, but I have no idea where they are. If they come to your place, and don't tell me where you are in case someone is listening in, but tell them nothing."

"But why? What has she done?"

Jake gave her the abridged version of the divorce, abuse, Russian Mafia, and Nathan being charged for her murder. "And now he has fled the country in search of her."

"No wonder she's so skittish. Poor girl."

"That poor girl is now one of the richest women in America, thanks to Power Lotto that reached a billion dollars two months ago. She has that lottery ticket stashed in a safe deposit box in some little town in Missouri, and the ex is wanting his share. Since she didn't cash in on it before the divorce, he doesn't get a dime. However, she needs to wait a while to make sure there's no hiccups with the divorce papers."

"And I'm assuming there is."

"Possibly. The divorce decree never made it to Meredith's attorney in spite of being signed by the court. I contacted her attorney of record, and he had an unfortunate car accident several days ago involving a train. His car stalled on the tracks. Police say it's suspicious, but the investigation is ongoing. The only reason he hadn't sent it to her was because he left on vacation shortly after the divorce trial. He told his secretary he wished to handle this one himself."

"Isn't that a little odd?"

"Very. Turns out the lawyer, like her ex-husband, also had some gambling debts. It's my guess she confided in him, not knowing she was waving a red cape in front of a bull. Anyway, my sources spotted the Russians with Nathan when they landed in Belize City. They're hunting Meredith to get that ticket. The banker and his family have been put in protective custody, so, for now, they're safe, as is the ticket."

"I can't send someone up there, Jake. You know how treacherous that road can be in good weather, much less a hurricane."

"I know. I'll keep trying to reach him. Can you do the same on your end? I'm already on my way. At least I can make it part of the way. All flights are grounded in Mexico and Central America but should be better by tomorrow."

"Thank you, Jake. I'll keep trying, too. Be safe."

"Yes, ma'am."

CHAPTER 24

The fire, although small, warmed them enough to fight off hyperthermia. Axel kept an eye on Meredith as her eyelids drooped and an occasional yawn escaped. Keeping the conversation going wasn't easy for him. He was used to being alone with his own thoughts. Even though he forced her to talk, it wasn't enough. Finally, he had leaned her back against the rock wall of the cave before building up the fire. When her head gently lay on his shoulder, he slipped his arm around her in hopes of keeping them both warm.

The howling wind, flickering fire, and the drip of rain into invisible pools in the darkest part of their refuge created a perfect combination to lull him toward sleep. Periodically, he touched her neck and, once, dared to slip his hand inside the waterproof jacket to her shoulder. The warmth indicated she was going to be okay enough that he let his eyes close to rest just a short while.

When something moved across his chest, he startled

awake, to find Meredith's head had moved onto his chest and her hand stretched out along his side in an embrace. A tenacle of smoke twisted upward from their fire, but the press of Meredith's nearness chased away any lingering chill in his body. He discovered she was held in place by his hand on her back and the other on her hip.

The morning light filtered through the tangled vines, causing wavy lines as tropical breezes pushed into the cave. Sounds of birds had returned, along with the gentle movement of water over cliffs that circled their grotto location. He wasn't sure he could move after sitting in one place so long and needed to move Meredith. Turning his head toward her, he could smell the remnants of what must have been flowery shampoo in her damp hair. The softness of her begged to be touched, but that was the last thing she needed after the last few tumultuous days.

He adjusted his sitting position, causing her to waken and stir. Using her hands, she pushed away then stretched. Although awkward, he managed to right himself and stand to his feet. He, too, needed to stretch. The night before, he'd made several cups of bitter coffee, and they'd feasted on beef jerky. There wasn't much, but it was enough to keep them satisfied until they could do better.

Meredith tried to stand but groaned at the stiffness in her legs. "I feel like I'm a hundred."

He reached down and pulled her to a standing position. Instantly, she put up her hands against his chest to push away as if it might be a reflex. The response didn't surprise or disappoint him. They were moving, side by side now, in a totally different direction than when they first met. The thought of how rude and curt he'd been to her made him wonder why she should trust him at all. But he knew they were both trying, in spite of their issues.

Sonya had done a number on him, along with Hollywood. Before that, it was his experiences in Afghanistan: trusting people who would turn around and try to kill you. If it hadn't been for Sister Elena, it was hard to say what would have happened to him. She was his lifeline, his anchor. He would forever be in her debt. She'd even taken in some of his army buddies. They'd come together to build something amazing in the jungle. Hopefully, the hurricane hadn't destroyed all the time, effort, and money that had gone into his slice of heaven. He wanted this to help other veterans and Sister Elena as well.

"If it's all right with you, let's hike out of here and get to my place. I'm anxious to take a look at the damage." He slipped on his backpack and reached for hers, but she grabbed it first.

"I can do this. If I need help, I promise, I'll ask," she said, slipping her arms through the straps. "Ready," she said with a nod as she grabbed the straps that now came across his shoulders. "I want to see your Shangri-La."

"Keep in mind it isn't finished," he said, pushing the vines aside. "Welcome to Finallea."

"Finallea? As in we're finally here?" she stepped outside and caught her breath. "Is this the same place we were yesterday?"

"Exactly," he chuckled. "The same. I knew the water would run down quickly. Storm blew out of here about seven last night."

He watched as her face lit up with awe. The

turquoise pools appeared serene now and gently flowed toward a waterfall that had transformed from monster to tame as it spilled gently over the edge into a series of more pools. The final destination would be the ocean. Although some downed branches reflected the storm, the steep rock formations protected many of the beautiful trees and flowers that grew profusely in this part of the jungle.

"It's beautiful, Axel." She turned to him and offered a wide, childlike smile. "I can't wait to see the rest."

He tilted his head toward their destination. "Shouldn't be far if we don't run into much downed debris. Of course, if we traveled by road, the trip would be easier. We're safer going forward this way."

She saluted him. "We've come this far. No turning back."

"No turning back," he echoed with pleasure.

Their trek lasted longer than Axel intended, but Meredith kept stopping to ask questions about things she was seeing for the first time. Everything interested or surprised her, and he didn't want to squash that kind of enthusiasm. Besides, it was nice to have someone appreciate this side of Belize for a change.

Along with the dangers of downed vegetation, there was always the unexpected appearance of a lost jaguar or ocelot. Normally, they were not going to approach or attack, but they would be dealing with loss of habitat, too. Their patience would be tested, and they might be hungry. He'd never seen any crocodiles in the area, but storm surge may have changed that.

The last steep climb took them to a ridge that overlooked his compound. There were more downed limbs and signs of possible storm surge, but even from here, he could tell no real damage had been done. Everything appeared to be in tack from the outside. Fingers crossed it would also be true for the inside and the systems that ran the place. The solar roof tiles remained secure but warranted a closer inspection once they arrived.

"You built this?" Meredith gasped.

"I had some help from a few army buddies. They needed a distraction, and free was about what I could afford after buying supplies and getting Sister Elena squared away with a new place for the children and her clinic. It's been a slow process, mostly because I can only do so much by myself."

They started their descent as the sounds of the jungle forced Meredith to keep making sudden stops and grabbing his arm. "What was that?"

"Howler monkey. Loud, aren't they?" he laughed. "See that," he asked, pointing to a bird with bright red, blue, and yellow feathers decorating a head to tail length that approached thirty-two inches. "Scarlet macaw."

"I've seen them in the zoo but never like this."

"They can live to be forty years old. They're a protected species, but there are always poachers trying to make a buck." The joy in her eyes touched him deeply. He tried to talk to Sonya once about his dream for this place. She was always too busy to come see it, or wanted to wait until it was finished with all the amenities. Once he told her there probably wouldn't be many, she lost interest. Maybe that's when he decided to quit Hollywood.

Once on level ground, he could see there would be some cleanup but nothing major. He led Meredith into one of the huts and said he wanted to make sure there were no four-legged visitors taking refuge from the storm. He was grateful the storm was only a category one and had come ashore a little farther up the shoreline. Didn't mean it wasn't serious. The people over the mountains in Guatemala would suffer the most.

He returned to see Meredith standing outside, her face twisted in fear at something out of his line of sight. He grabbed his sawed-off shotgun from its hiding place and checked to make sure it was loaded. Could be a big cat came calling and had her frozen in place. He edged closer to the door, and that's when he saw her lift her arms in surrender, followed by a male voice.

~ ~ ~ ~

Nathan watched his two Russian companions' scarf down a heavy breakfast that many would have called a heart attack on a plate. They spoke in their own language and occasionally glanced his way then spoke from the corner of a full mouth, followed by a snicker. They were brutes. Although they dressed in suits and ties back home, they dressed like locals here with flowery shirts and T-shirts advertising sea turtles or barrier reef tours, among other tourist destinations. He refused to be that casual but did dress down a bit.

Besides, he was sure Sonya Lavenworth preferred men who didn't resemble a tourist on some kind of jungle cruise. However, she did have a fling with that rough character who took celebrities into the wild and, apparently, was even engaged to him. What would a fine specimen like her want with a slug like Axel

Cahill?

Women. Always on the lookout for romance with a pirate or a misunderstood billionaire. Maybe that Axel character was really a straight-up guy who just played the part in a better-safe-than-sorry storyline.

He replayed her interview in his head from the day before. Everyone was hunkered down in the resort, which made a perfect dramatic backdrop for a movie star the world loved. Before she went to the interview, Sonya invited him to an early happy hour with enough finger food to keep him from having to buck up for dinner. She smiled a lot, giving him a warm-all-over feeling, and wondered if she had this kind of effect on every man she met. Clearly that Axel character didn't.

Then the questions began after he'd had a couple of drinks, which he was all too happy to answer. She'd barely touched hers, he noticed. It felt like a gentle interrogation. Maybe it was the candlelight or the sound of rain and wind, but he was feeling pretty good about himself. With the undivided attention he was getting from her, maybe he could be her knight in shining armor during this difficult breakup.

"So, you mean to tell me, your wife—I'm sorry, ex-wife, pretended to be dead and left you on the hook for murder? That's horrible. She seemed a bit elusive when we met. I think she knew Axel had money and was trying to lure him into thinking she was some kind of innocent and helpless woman who needed his help. He was always a sucker for those kinds of people."

"That doesn't sound like Meredith." Even though things hadn't worked out between them, he knew her to be a good woman. She'd put up with him a lot longer than he deserved. "Whatever the reason, I'm here to bring her back to clear my name. And she owes me a lot of money. I intend to get it."

"I suppose the gentlemen who keep hovering around you offered to help with that task."

"Yes. They are in finance and say I have a right to the money."

"I'm sure they did. And they'll get a cut, no doubt."

Nathan grimaced. "Unfortunately. However, I can't get to that little town. What was it? Turtle Bay? From the way you described it, sounds like a hole in the wall. This hurricane has probably ruined any chance of surprising her."

"It'll be out of here in no time. Besides, I seriously doubt she's there, if she wants to hide from you, and I'm sure she knows you're here by now since the news is everywhere of our breakup. Axel will have taken her to his little compound in the jungle. Hideous place. Wild animals, no air-conditioning, and certainly no amenities. Just another reminder why I broke it off." She took a deep breath and let it out slowly. "That and he was a cheater." She laid a hand on his. "I hate to tell you this, but Axel and Meredith were having an affair."

It shouldn't have surprised him that Meredith needed or even wanted someone else. But it did. He figured after all he'd put her through, she'd be more hesitant to get involved with anyone else. Yes, he'd lost his temper a few times and hurt her, but he hadn't meant to do it. She forgave him at first then toughened up enough to start over, leaving him to pick up the pieces—alone. Well, why wouldn't she with all that money she was hoarding.

Her assistant showed up and told her it was time for the interview. Sonya stood and kissed him on the cheek.

"You're a dear, Nathan. I'm hoping this is all a big misunderstanding. Maybe she'll come running back to you after she sees what a cad Axel Cahill really is."

"Will you take Axel back?" he asked.

She arched an eyebrow. "Don't be ridiculous."

CHAPTER 25

Standing no more than twenty feet away was a group of seven men. One moved forward, like a stalking jaguar, never taking his eyes off Meredith. In one hand was a machete; the other held a rifle. His dark hair was partially pulled back into a topknot; the rest seemed to fall down his back. The wide, narrow eyes were outlined in a thick band of black then trailed down his cheeks into a hook shape. Tattoos of an ancient design covered his shoulders and arms.

Although his chest and torso were bare, only a loincloth covered his lower extremities. His followers stood behind him, their heads constantly turning, as if expecting trouble. The brown skin of his legs, covered in black spots, resembled that of a jaguar. The oddest thing about him was the pattern of red smeared over his entire chest. Then she noticed a hole on the upper right side that oozed blood.

His thick lips pooched out as he turned his head slightly, careful not to take his eyes off her as he spoke to his men in a language she didn't understand. Cocking his head again, he examined her from head to toe. Meredith understood she was in serious trouble. They all took a step closer then she heard a familiar voice.

"Hold it right there, Buluc."

Axel emerged from the side of one of the huts. Buluc's men jumped to attention as they raised their machetes and rifles toward him. But the leader lifted his chin and said something to put them at ease.

"Put your weapons down now, or I may need to put another hole in your chest. Not sure you can take another one. You're bleeding way too much. My friend here is a doctor. Well, maybe not quite a doctor, but she works at the new clinic in Turtle Bay. Let her check you out."

Buluc took another invasive look at Meredith, waiting for her to respond. She stepped off the deck toward him. "He's right. I have some medical supplies in my bag. Can I see the wound?"

The Mayan remained poised as a threat but nodded slowly as he kept his weapons.

"No. Stay there," Axel ordered Meredith. "He can bleed out for all I care if he doesn't drop those weapons," he said, waving her back. "Now, be a good boy and do what I say."

"I will not."

"Then get off my land. You're dripping blood and it will attract predators—the four-legged kind. I don't want any trouble."

"We will take the woman. There is only one of you."

"True. You are in no shape to take her." He focused on the others. "I can take several of you out before you get close to my friend. And, Buluc, you'll be the first to fall."

Buluc appeared to try and grin when his weapons fell out of his hands and his knees buckled. Before he hit the ground, Axel tossed his weapon to one of the other men and gathered Buluc up in his arms like a baby. "I gotcha. Meredith, inside. He's in bad shape. There's a large dining room table."

Meredith ran ahead of him and into the dining area. The table was empty, and she quickly ran her finger across it, finding a layer of grime. She searched under the sink and found a container of disinfectant wipes. Axel was walking through the door as she mopped the surface the best she could.

"I need you to get my backpack. There are medical supplies in there. If you have anything, I'll need that, too." The other men peered in the windows that circled the dining area. They were fierce with their painted faces and tattoos; some had their hair down and others, up in a topknot like Buluc. The piercing stares of mistrust reminded her of her own issues, and she wondered if others saw her like these men: angry and ready to attack or bolt, depending on the circumstance.

Laid on the table, the warrior grimaced but didn't so much as moan. Axel squeezed her arm in reassurance. "I'll get the supplies." He turned to the men standing at the windows. "We'll take good care of him."

A couple nodded and another one gave a thumbs-up, which surprised Meredith as Axel left her alone. She bent closer to Buluc and felt his head. He was burning up.

"I'm Meredith."

The man let his gaze go around her face then lifted his arm from the elbow. She grasped his hand and felt the strength in his grip. Patting his hand with her free one, she laid his clammy palm on the table. "I'm glad you found us in time."

Although his stare remained penetrating and unnerved her, it wasn't all that different than a gang member coming into the ER with a gunshot wound. Well, except she was limited on what she had available to treat him, and it was a lot more sterile than this place after a hurricane. Before she had time to wonder how this would end, Axel hurried back in and placed her backpack on the end of the table, along with a burlap bag of miscellaneous items.

"Let me know how I can help, Meredith. I had some training with the Green Berets when I served with the military."

She jerked around to stare at him, surprised at this new information. "Well, first thing you can do is squirt that hand sanitizer on my hands and give me some of the gloves in that plastic bag. Then you do the same."

Before she ever finished speaking, he squirted the clear liquid into her hands.

Once they were both gloved, she continued. "Let's see what we got here, Buluc," she said matter-of-factly.

Cleaning his chest, the cool temperature of the alcohol poured on the sponges and applied to his skin caused him discomfort. She moved her hands carefully in case there were other injuries. Other than some scrapes, there was nothing serious. Then she cleaned the area with the hole the size of a silver dollar. The skin was inflamed, and blood continued to flow.

"Buluc, how did you get this wound?" she asked, holding her hands away from the damaged area.

"I go into the storm to help my family find cover.

When I did, the wind blew something into my shoulder. I pulled it out."

"What was it?" she continued.

"It was a pointed piece of fence that had come loose from the ground where my wife kept her pig."

"So, you're telling me the thing that rammed into your body was from a pigpen?"

"Yes."

"And you walked here to steal from me? Take my supplies?" Axel fumed. "No wonder Buluc Chabtan was angry with you."

"I need to take a closer look. It's already infected. Probably had pig feces and who knows what else on it before it slammed into his chest. Buluc, this is going to hurt." She dropped what appeared to be large tweezers into a saucer and poured peroxide over them.

"I am strong," he huffed.

"We'll see about that," Axel said, handing him a bottle of Jack Daniels. "Drink this my friend, because she is going to make you cry like a baby." He helped him take several swallows before lowering his shoulders again.

Meredith had dumped the contents of her backpack among the items Axel retrieved. Fortunately, there was some wound cleanser with his things. She wasn't sure why he had this kind of thing with his supplies, but she was glad he did.

"Pour the whiskey in the wound. It will be enough," Buluc ordered.

She proceeded to spray the area. "I will not. I'd use it in a pinch though." She now had a clear view of the open wound. "This is going to hurt, Buluc. You might want to drink more of that whiskey before I start digging around in there." She nodded toward a large pair of tweezers in the saucer then at Buluc. "He probably needs a little more happy juice to be medicated enough. We'll save the rest in case we need it."

Axel did as she asked then gave the bottle back to Buluc. He motioned for one of his men to come help the Mayan raise up enough to drink. He pulled her aside but remained near, even though it might be closer than she appreciated. Yet, she didn't shy away but stared up into his eyes as if waiting for instructions.

"Just want to make sure you're okay. Buluc can be a mean SOB, but don't let him rattle you. I won't let him hurt you."

She sighed then took a big breath. "Are you sure about that? Those other men seem to be pretty dangerous, too. I've treated gunshot wounds of gang members in the ER, but I had police with big guns standing by. Here, I've got you and howler monkeys."

"Don't underestimate the monkeys." He raised his chin toward Buluc's men. "I know these guys. You fix him up, and he'll be a force to be reckoned with, even if the Russian army comes searching for you. Mayan warriors can be fierce against an enemy. It won't take them long to realize you're not one of the bad guys."

"I think I left all my antibiotics with Sister Elena for the children. He's going to need some ASAP when I'm finished poking around on him. He's running a fever. Do you have anything? I know you off-the-grid guys sometimes have something called chitin."

"And how would you know that?"

Her mouth turned up on one corner. "I admit I

googled you after I found out who you were. I'm very curious about alternative medicine, and I read an article where you used it on one of your guests who got hurt."

"Yeah. I got some in my stash. Pays to be prepared around here. You do know it's made from the shells of crustaceans. That doesn't bother you that it might not be safe?"

"Using an antibiotic on a man who has never had any might also be dangerous. Besides, I need to stop the bleeding. I know once it is made into a powder, it can be used as hemostatic dressing. It also has antimicrobial properties that can help with infection, so get it for me please."

He couldn't help but search her face and admitted silently that he was in love with the woman. Beauty and brains wasn't something he had seen much of in Hollywood. And if he did, there was always a catch or a sacrifice to your moral fiber. Tangled hair, smelling like a two-day hike on rough terrain, no makeup, and she stood like a goddess with a plan to save a life.

"What?" she snapped. Her body language spoke defense.

He took a step closer, and she stiffened, arms dropped to her side. "I was just thinking you are the most tenacious and beautiful woman I've ever met."

"I would kiss you right now for thinking that out loud, but every one of your friends are staring at us."

He turned around to see curious eyes studying them. They probably had never seen him with a woman before.

"Maybe you should go get the chitin. Buluc appears to be feeling pretty mellow."

"The way they're undressing you with those

inappropriate stares, I'm thinking I need to mark my territory." He jerked her into his arms and kissed her long and hard. When he released her, she blinked several times and tried to catch her breath.

"Consider your territory pleasantly marked," she said, trying to catch her breath.

CHAPTER 26

Meredith could smell the cooking in the kitchen as Axel conversed with several of Buluc's men who had come inside earlier to help hold their leader down as she dug into his wound. Even though he'd had enough whiskey to knock a normal human out, he remained drowsy enough to kick and squirm as she removed the shrapnel found in his significant wound.

The supplies Axel brought her included acetaminophen for pain and fever. Buluc responded well to that and, now, rested quietly on the table. She hoped to have him moved within the hour if beds had been made with clean sheets. The wound itself wasn't nearly as bad as she first thought, but could still be a killer. It was a good thing he'd found them when he had.

Axel promised to keep an eye on him while he fixed everyone a meal if she wanted to explore the compound. First, she made sure there was a clean place for her patient to heal and found that this main building had three bedrooms and two bathrooms, one of which came with an outdoor shower. The common area included the kitchen, dining, and living room area. So much was open to the outside that she enjoyed moving in and out of the house into the gardens and patio area. Screens could be lowered easily enough in all the rooms.

The sounds of the ocean were close, and she ventured toward the pounding waves just beyond the palms that towered beneath the emergent layer of the rainforest. She hadn't expected them to be so tall. A few appeared damaged, but, luckily, this part of the country hadn't been hit hard. Mostly, there had been rain. Storm surge had not reached Finallea, as Axel called it, and for that she was glad. The compound was a good ten feet above sea level here, so she hoped this had been a good location for what he was trying to do.

"Hungry?" She whirled around to see Axel standing like a statue, as if he'd been watching her.

Several times, she thought he had been observing her behind those mirrored sunglasses he wore over the last week. That wasn't possible during the hurricane, but now, with the storm gone, she figured he'd worn them when they left the cave to appraise her without being obvious. But, for now, they were on top of his head. She could see the blue of his eyes and the creases at the corners that gave his angled face more character. He'd changed into some clean clothes that were faded and sported a few rips and holes that somehow gave him a cool vibe. Although they were far from wrinkle-free, they still managed to give him a rugged and carefree appearance.

"Yes, I'm starved. How's our patient?"

"Starting to come to and moaning very loudly. In spite of his name, he's a big baby."

"His name?"

"Yeah, his whole name is Buluc Chabtan. Named after the Mayan god of war, violence, and sudden death. People prayed to him for success in war. They thought by doing that it would help them stay on his good side. Oh, and avoid sudden death. Buluc likes to scare tourists, and wannabe cartel guys with stories that blood was seen as nourishment for the gods and a human life was the ultimate gift to a deity. Whether he's ever acted on that—I don't want to know."

Meredith chuckled. "I'm glad you didn't tell me that before I made him mad by digging in that wound. He should be fine by the way, although I really think seeing a doctor would be a good idea, and maybe getting antibiotics if possible."

"Won't happen. He rarely leaves the jungle." He pointed toward the mountains from which they'd come. "Buluc and his men protect this part of the jungle. It's actually protected by the government, but there are always poachers, drug mules, and tourists searching for unscripted adventure that can cause harm to the environment. Not to mention bring disease and the ways of the outside world to his village. He has a reputation, and outsiders don't mess with him."

"How is it you're friends?"

They started back toward the compound.

"The short version is he knows I'm making this place to educate people about biodiversity, and bring veterans down here to heal in the process. With any luck, some will stay and help out. Like to give them a job and a purpose. When you showed up, I thought maybe these people could finally have some health care they wouldn't be afraid of. Doubt they'd come into town, but they might let you come visit them." He grinned. "Well, unless Buluc is crazy mad when he gets on his feet."

"So, you're using me for your project's success," she said drily.

He stopped suddenly and faced her. "Maybe. It does sound like that, I know. I have a lot riding on this project. Believe it or not, even I want to make a difference. I hoped when you saw it, knew my plan, you'd decide to stay."

"Of course, you also know I have enough money to make this project happen as well. Too bad you didn't tell me about it before you knew my secret."

"Well since you reminded me of another spoiled, self-absorbed woman who just might be using the only family I've ever known to aid their agenda, I wouldn't have told you anything but hit the road. Which I believe I did from the start."

"Nice your buddy Stateside had access to finding out about me."

"He painted a far different picture of you than was true. I'm sorry about that."

"I bet," she said, stepping around him. "I guess this is what I should expect from now on."

"Yes, you should." He hurried around her to cut off the retreat without touching her, which would only have thrown gas on a smoldering fire. "There is always going to be someone who pretends to be something they're not because you're rich. You're going to get hit with a lot of oh-poor-me stories: my child needs a kidney but I don't have the money, send me to college, blah, blah,

blah. You're going to be romanced, lied to, and forced to believe the unbelievable for the rest of your life or until the money is gone. So, you'd better find a place to hide like I have. And just so you know, I don't want or need your money." He took a step closer to her, unaware of how angry he looked until she took a step back. "I have plenty. Yes, I am strapped for cash right now because I had to pay off that medical clinic Sister Elena insisted on because if I didn't, the bank was going to come calling and close her down and take everything. The bishop would have been thrilled not to have to worry about it anymore or about her. She's a troublemaker." He pointed toward the compound. "That can wait. I thought you were different. Guess I was wrong." He turned away then back. "Oh, and just so you'll be on the lookout, guys saying 'I thought you were different. I was wrong,' is a warning to leave. You know—like me. Thanks for screwing my head up, Meredith."

He was a self-made man and no stranger to adversity. Until she won the lottery, she would have considered him wealthy beyond anything she could imagine. What he'd done with his earnings was exactly what she wanted to do. Use her talents to help others. The strength she experienced when he held her in his arms chased all the nightmares away from the last few years. He had asked for nothing from her nor even insinuated he needed financial support from her. All he'd done was share his life and dream with her because—he trusted her with the knowledge. What had she done? Showed him Sonya Lavenworth and herself were cut from the same cloth.

Watching him run up onto the deck as the interior

lights came on, she hurried to join him. Apologizing wouldn't be easy, but he deserved it. She hoped it wasn't too late to start over and admit her feelings and trust issues blinded her to who he really was: a good man. She broke into a run, expecting the opportunity to evaporate before she even joined him. Then he ran outside.

"Meredith," he yelled. "Meredith, I need your help."

She was already running up on the deck before he spotted her.

"What's wrong?"

"I don't know. Buluc. I think he's convulsing."

~ ~ ~ ~

Hours later, the sound of rain woke Axel in the middle of the night. He'd stretched out on his bed without bothering to make it. The job of lowering the screens and checking to make sure that nothing loose would catch on a stiff breeze went quickly with Buluc's men helping him out. They bedded down in the small bedroom on the floor. The third bedroom was for Buluc. His fever had spiked, and Meredith thought the quick seizure was from that. His blood pressure was also low but normalized within fifteen minutes.

The men carried him to the outdoor shower attached to the bathroom. With so many bodies in such a small space, it was a miracle she could turn on the water to cover him. Everyone got soaking wet, including Meredith, who kept bathing his head and wound. Once inside, she toweled him off carefully.

Watching her treat the Mayan was hypnotic for Axel, as she talked softly to him and patted him with dry towels. Once he stabilized, Buluc never took his eyes off her as her hands once more applied the chitin to the hole in his upper chest and shoulder. She would softly reassure him. At one point, she moved his hair away from his face, causing his eyes to crease at the corners.

"I will stay with you, Buluc, all night. Are you okay with that?" she'd asked.

The other men chuckled, speaking in their Mayan tongue, nodding and elbowing each other. Buluc finally closed his eyes and whispered, "Yes."

It was nearly midnight when Axel came to tell her everything was locked up tight. "I put some folded sheets at the foot of my bed. I'll stay with him. Get some sleep." He wanted to apologize for his earlier behavior, but that wasn't something that came easy for him lately. The thought of her leaving weighed on him, but she was going to have to find her own way to him if this relationship had a chance of working.

She sat in a folding chair, leaning forward, staring at Buluc. "I would feel much better if I had a tetanus shot to give him."

"I'm pretty sure the fire department would have one. The paramedics are also based there. I'm guessing he's never had one before. Might be okay. These people don't know anything about stuff like that."

"Maybe I could go back and try to get one," she said calmly then met his eyes.

He squatted down beside her and placed his hand on the back of her chair. "Meredith, that's a bad idea. If people are hunting for you, then that is a risky move. If you think it's that important, I'll go. I can navigate this jungle faster than you. Just tell me what you need, and

I'll get it."

"What I need," she said, placing her hand on his cheek, "is for you to forgive me for all those things I said. What you have here is the beginning of something wonderful. I wanted this to be a new beginning for me, about all I've done is make things worse. I wish I had never won the money. It's not like I earned it. If I can just take care of Sister Elena and the children with it, then I can say I did something worthwhile in my life."

"Forgiven," he said, placing his hand on hers. "You're going to have to stay because I think the way Buluc was looking at you, you might be engaged now."

"Well, he would be better than the last guy I married," she admitted. "I promised I'd stay here with him. But I would love a shower and clean clothes."

"I've got some clothes my friends left here when they helped me build this place. I'm sure I've got something to cinch it tighter until your clothes dry." He stood and pulled her up. "I'll lay the clothes on my bed then come back until you're ready. You haven't eaten anything, so I'll bring you some soup."

She nodded and started to turn away when he reached out and took her hand. "Meredith, I'm also sorry about in the kitchen earlier when I made that crack about marking my territory. Now that I think about it, I realize it sounded pretty chauvinistic. I forced myself on you, and my timing was way off. You just were so damn pretty standing there staring out the window and"—he paused— "it made me happy to have you here."

"I am happy to be here. I love it, Axel. I guess that scared me a little because I certainly wasn't wanting any kind of relationship, and then you walk in like you just jumped off the cover of a romance novel."

He couldn't help but grin at her description, considering he was rather rough around the edges when it came to romance. "I want to get you through this so you can see your way to the future. You're always welcome here, and certainly at the orphanage. No pressure on my part."

"I'm not one of your celebrity rescues, but I appreciate the effort it took to rescue me from all this."

"It's what I do," he said, tilting his head to inspect her closer. "Besides, I'm not sure who rescued who in this case."

Meredith took his free hand and, for a few moments, they gazed into each other's eyes, unsure of what to say next, until she stepped forward and embraced him gently, turned, and disappeared toward the shower.

CHAPTER 27

After reflecting back on their talk several hours earlier, Axel padded into where Meredith watched over Buluc. He was determined this time he'd make her go to bed for a while. She'd left the robe he'd hung in the shower on a hanger in the open space used as a closet. The scrub-like outfit had replaced her clothes after she managed to rinse hers to hang in the closet. The rain was steady and just the kind of night he liked to sleep in, in the jungle. The voices in the next room cautioned him as he approached.

Meredith was taking Buluc's temperature, speaking in the soothing voice she used on patients. He'd heard the same tone when she'd taken care of the twins. The sound was comforting and melodic. The Mayan was now sitting up in bed sipping from a cup she held to his lips. His eyes never left her, and Axel couldn't help but wonder what was going through the man's head. Hopefully, it wasn't anything he would have to fight him over. That was one confrontation he might not be able to win, even if the man was wounded.

"Meredith, why don't you get some sleep?" he asked, walking in then leaning on a chair with his arms folded across his chest. "I can take care of this guy."

"I don't want or need you to be here with me. I want Meredith. Get lost." He waved toward the door with his one good arm. She had already put the other in a sling.

"I'd say you're better, Buluc. You've been a lot of trouble," Axel snapped as he walked around to the other side of the bed. "How soon can he go?" he asked drily, deliberately avoiding eye contact with the Mayan.

"When I am ready, Axel," Buluc responded then turned a warm expression on Meredith. "I might need extra care for a while."

"It's important you let this heal and not get the wound dirty. Maybe some sunshine will help. But I am tired, Buluc. Would you mind if I take a short nap? I will be close by. Just call me."

"No need of that. I'll be here," Axel said with a frown and arched an eyebrow at the Mayan then at Meredith. "I made the bed. Take as long as you need."

Buluc waved again at the door. "Yes, Meredith. As long as you need."

She reached down and felt his head for a temperature again, making him grin broadly as he switched his attention to Axel. "No fever. I won't be long, my friend. You are in good hands."

Buluc narrowed his eyes at Axel. "I'm not so sure of that."

Axel let a sinister chuckle loose deep in his throat to send the man a message he wasn't afraid of him.

~ ~ ~ ~

Meredith stretched several times before she opened her eyes to the sound of birds outside her window. A tropical breeze moved palms to create dancing shadows across the walls. Rolling to her back, she studied the plain room and enjoyed the feeling of freedom. The distant sound of waves crashing against the shore nearly lulled her back to sleep.

The aroma of coffee gave her strength to push back the sheet and stand, only to stretch again. Stepping into the small hall, she realized no one was moving about inside the house. She peeked inside Buluc's room and discovered him gone. Entering the common area, she spotted the coffeepot. There was a clean empty mug waiting for her with a container of nondairy creamer to the side. Pouring herself a cup of coffee, she spotted the others sitting outside, eating breakfast.

"There she is," called Buluc. "I was worried." He struggled to get up from the Adirondack chair because of one arm being in a sling. "Join us." He motioned for her to sit in his chair, and she noticed Axel was nowhere to be found. "Axel took his boat back to his town," Buluc informed her. "Said he wanted to check on the nun and children. He also said I needed some kind of shot to protect me, but I am strong enough."

"How long will he be gone?"

"The sea is calm now, so by afternoon. My men will stay to protect you." He puffed out his chest as did a few others who nodded agreement as they put a fist to their chest. "No worries. Do you want to feel my head?" he asked as he lowered his face close to hers.

She laid a palm on his forehead and smiled. "Very

good. I need to check you over in a bit to make sure there isn't more infection. How do you feel?"

He straightened and put on a fierce expression. "Like the mighty Buluc Chabtan, the Mayan god of war." He cocked his head and closed one eye. "Are you impressed?"

"Very. Must be why you made such a remarkable recovery." Part of her wanted to giggle at his theatrical show of strength. Even though he remained menacing, she doubted Axel would have left her alone with these men if he hadn't trusted them with her safety.

"The great Buluc Chabtan must have sent you to heal me." His voice was matter-of-fact as he took in a deep breath. "I owe you a great debt."

"Okay. Now sit down and rest. Then you'll need to take a nap."

One of his men pulled up another chair next to hers for Buluc as the breezes swept across the deck. The palm fronds waved, letting the sun in and out across them. The men asked her many questions about where she was from, her medicine, why she came to Belize, and a few personal questions as well.

"Are you Axel's woman?" Buluc asked with a serious tone.

"We are very good friends. Where I'm from, women don't feel they need a man to take care of them."

"I see," he said, tapping his finger against his chin. "But here, that is not possible. You need a man. Would you like for me to find you one?"

"I would not. I had one man, and it didn't work out."

"Yes. Yes. Axel said this husband was not worthy."

"He said that?" she said with a slight intake of breath to imitate shock.

"Not in so many words, but if we must stay here to protect you, I think you did not make a good decision in choosing a husband. I have done this many times. Never have I made a mistake in finding a suitable mate. I would offer myself, but I already have a wife."

"Good to know."

"It is customary to have a matchmaker. I will be yours."

"Oh goodie," she said, rolling her eyes. "I think I'll just not get married."

"No. We have accepted you as one of our own."

The other men bobbed their heads in agreement.

"We follow the old ways here in Belize. Well, as much as possible. The young ones think they know better."

"And if they don't fall into line?"

He shrugged. "Then we beat them. Kill them, maybe." His bottom lip protruded a bit.

Meredith gasped and turned sideways in her chair to glare at him. Then they all laughed as he poked her in the arm with his good hand.

"I am making a joke. We let them go, but they always come back. Living in the jungle among the people of their ancestry is a religious experience. I am thinking that maybe Axel needs a woman. I have told him this many times. You are the first one he has brought here. That is a good sign. Do you know if Axel has a dowry he can use for a wife?"

It was all she could do to keep from laughing out loud. "No. I'm sorry. I don't know. Is that important?"

"Not so much these days, but among my village, my family, we still insist on it. The married couple will live with the woman's family for six to seven years. But I am flexible on this. Since you have no family here, Axel would not have to work for your parents. I think maybe this place might be good enough to live."

"I see you've given this a great deal of thought."

"Yes. It is important to me that you are well taken care of. Once you marry Axel, if it pleases you to follow our ways, you may live with my family or here. I will serve as your father."

Meredith wanted to remind him he was most likely not old enough to be her father. "You have given me a lot to think about, Buluc. Thank you for caring about my welfare."

He bowed his head and laid his hand on his heart. "It is my honor."

Pushing out of the chair, she extended a hand to him. "Now, I need to check you out to make sure all is well."

"I will then take a nap and, when that is done, we will wait a little while longer for Axel to return. I will speak to him about all these things. Then we will leave."

"You're the boss," she said, coaxing him to follow her inside.

"I am also a god."

"Yes. That, too." Meredith decided agreeing with him on most of his ideas would keep things moving in the right direction. Hoping Axel would hurry back, she wished now she'd never mentioned the tetanus shot.

~ ~ ~ ~

The waves were a little choppy when Axel sailed into port. Since his dock was the farthest out, he didn't expect anyone to notice him. A number of people were taking care of their boats, checking to see if there was damage that needed attention. Most of these boats were fishing boats. He had purchased one of those a number of years ago and had transformed it into one to take tourists out to the Barrier Reef Reserve when he needed some easy money.

He didn't like dipping into his reserve unless it was for Sister Elena. Unfortunately, over the last year, that had been a monthly extraction that sucked the life out of the reserves. She was right about one thing. They needed a miracle to keep the orphanage afloat. Perish the thought, but he just might need to go back to work at his former reality TV program.

It had been a big money maker, both for him and the network. When he left, they made sure he knew, whenever he was ready, they would reboot the series. Even now, in syndication, the show had a big following here and internationally. That's how he'd been able to afford to live like he had for the last couple of years.

There wasn't a way to call Luis to see how things went with Sister Elena, since he'd lost his phone in their watery escape. The storm surge hadn't been much and didn't even reach the town—mostly rutted the beach, which was already being repaired. He wondered about his friend Juan and how his restaurant had faired.

Slipping through side streets and then taking a bicycle taxi, he hoped to keep the Russians, Nathan, and maybe that not-so-married couple, from spotting him. He kept his hat pulled down low on his forehead, wore sunglasses he'd found on the boat, and also some nondescript clothes he used when he went fishing. They didn't smell all that great, but maybe that would keep an interested party back enough to protect his identity.

His first stop was the fire station to pick up the tetanus shots for Buluc and his men. They had plenty to share, and he promised to restock for them when he returned. Even though the Mayans didn't appear to be injured, it might just be a good idea to vaccinate them, too. They lived a rough life protecting the jungle from would-be poachers and drug lords. Sometimes well-meaning environmentalists on college break did more harm than good. They also needed some serious intervention on their well-intended activities. Buluc loved scaring those do-gooders. Said if they would pick up after themselves, the environment would be just fine.

Taking the street behind the orphanage where a few home businesses operated, he got permission to slip through their back door and into the alley. Opening the gate, he could hear Luis's deep voice raised to its top volume. He stood in the kitchen, waving his arms then rubbing his face with both hands, followed by making the sign of the cross. A police officer stood patiently with his hands on his hips while children ran in and out of the kitchen. The officer didn't take notes but said something about being covered up with needy tourists. He'd do what he could and swing back around later to let him know what he found out. Luis kept complaining, kissing his fingers and lifting them toward Heaven as he followed the officer into the common area. With a sense of trouble brewing, he used the stealth moves he'd learned in the Green Berets to slip inside without detection. As he tried to move forward in order to listen to Luis, the twins came storming in with plans of their own.

"Luis made cookies. Let's get some." It was Pedro nodding to his twin as he climbed up on the counter toward the warm cookies spread out on cooling racks.

Axel moved closer, their attention totally devoted to stealing cookies.

"What do you think you're doing?" he asked firmly. Both children yelped, but Pedro lost his balance and toppled over the edge into Axel's waiting arms. "Were you stealing?" He set the little boy's bare feet onto the floor and made sure his disapproval showed in his eyes.

Rosa sighed and pretended to fall back against the cabinet in great dramatic flair. "Thank goodness, you're here, Axel. We thought we heard a rat that would steal those cookies." She lowered her gaze to the floor and puckered her lips. "The other children would have been so sad to not get a treat. We only came to rescue and protect them."

"The only rats in here are named Rosa and Pedro. You've just broken two commandments in less than a minute."

"Luis says possession is nine tenths of the law," Pedro said, shrugging his shoulders as if that might help his argument. "I'm not sure what that means though. But it sounded important. So maybe those commandments are okay." The little rascal looked at his sister who put her arm around him. She bobbed her head as if to prove they were in agreement.

"Come here," he said, scooping one up for each arm. They hugged his neck.

Luis walked in grumbling until he saw Axel. "I'm glad you're here." His voice quivered and sounded as if he might cry.

Axel set the children's feet on the floor and told them to go play, before turning back to Luis.

"What the hell happened? Why were the police

here?"

Luis collapsed onto a stool. "Sister Elena. She's gone. Those men who came for Meredith took her."

CHAPTER 28

By the time Axel had made a supply run and created a survival backpack, it was late afternoon. Enlisting the help of Hector, the hotel muscle who had given him his car, took a great deal of negotiations, but, in the end, he agreed to sail him to a cove where Axel could then hike back to the compound Finallea. The terrain was familiar, and he'd done it a number of times. He wasn't sure what the road conditions were after the torrential rain, and another car could possibly slow him down.

The section of ground that washed completely away concerned him. There was an easy way to go around it, but it meant leaving their vehicle and walking the rest of the way. To top it off, Sister Elena was with them. She wasn't a young woman and probably shouldn't be doing such a strenuous walk.

Nathan and the two Russians would find the car he left behind if they could make it that far in their own vehicle. He doubted it. There were going to be chunks of the road missing. That's why he had opted for the cave. It would have been too treacherous to hike all the way then have to turn back for the cave option. By then the hurricane could have blown them out to sea. According to Buluc's men, the road withstood the storm. He could almost hear Sister Elena declare it a miracle.

If they hurt her or caused her to come to harm in any way due to their reckless actions, they would pay the ultimate price. She was more than his spiritual advisor, which he often pretended to ignore, but also his adopted mother, advocate, cheerleader, and advisor. But mostly, she was his family. She was all he had. Putting her in peril flipped a dangerous switch deep inside him.

Once on land, he took mud and smeared on his face and other parts of his skin that clothing didn't cover. The military camo-green clothes and black boots went a long way to hide him. The tight black skull cap hid his blond hair. The last thing he added was night vision goggles, but he held off on pulling them down until it got completely dark. He hoped he could cut the Russians and Nathan off before they reached his compound in order to save Sister Elena.

If they managed to dodge enough potholes, debris on the road, and did not get lost, chances were good they might already be ahead of him. He would pick up their trail soon enough. Pressing on, he pondered the possibility they might make it to the compound before him. Meredith was tough when it came to taking care of others when they needed it most. Emotionally, he worried how she'd react when the ex-husband showed up to confront her or worse. Money could make a person do crazy things.

~ ~ ~ ~

Meredith didn't realize how much she'd been pacing until Buluc walked into the kitchen area and asked for some hot tea. The distraction was welcomed. Noticing the others outside, adjusting what little equipment they had, to head out, made her nervous to think they were leaving. Handing the cup to Buluc, he took it gingerly then stared at her over the rim as he took the first sip.

"Why are you nervous? You are making a hole in Axel's floor."

"Just concerned he's not back yet. Maybe something happened to him."

"Nothing happened to him. He'll come. My friends must go home to check on their families. I will stay with you until Axel returns. You do not need to be afraid."

"I'm not afraid. It's kind of you to wait, but if your family needs you, then please go check on them."

She glanced toward the deck and saw his men step off then disappear into the jungle. Soon, it would be dark. The sounds of the jungle would start and, without Axel, it would sound like they were under attack. The croak of tree frogs, the growl of hungry cats, and cracking branches that finally fell to the forest floor were reminders that this was a dangerous land. Add in a Mayan who believed himself a god made for an interesting sensation to add to all the others she'd experienced trying to find a new life.

Buluc didn't respond until he'd finished his tea. After setting his mug down, he adjusted the sling until he'd had enough then removed it. "I do not need this. I can't protect you with one arm. And my family will be taken care of by the others if something is needed." He walked outside to where his men had built a fire in the stone firepit. She reluctantly followed.

"I guess it's pointless to insist you put that back on?" She followed after him to the end of the deck. His attention focused on something through the sparse trees that led to the beach. He stood there statue still, listening, with an expression a god might actually call fire down from the sky and punish any would-be enemy.

"I'll warm up some of the soup Axel left for us. You need to keep up your strength if you plan on protecting me," she sighed.

"That would be good, woman."

He turned his head slightly so she could study the outline of his face. Such a beautiful man. Wild. Free. Terrifying. And most of all, a god. Inwardly, she felt amusement, although studying him from this distance, he kind of impressed her he might be able to call down the spirits when needed.

She cleared her throat making him turn farther around. "My name is Meredith, not woman."

One corner of his mouth started to lift then he seemed to think better of it and turned back around as if he'd lost interest. "Meredith, you may fix me food."

"Oh goodie," she groaned.

Without turning around, he spoke firmly. "Later, when I am full, you will tell me about your life."

"Later, when you are full, you can help me clean up the kitchen and wash dishes."

"Is this the reason you no longer have a man? He

would not wash dishes?" He turned to face her and walked back to tower over her.

"Among other things," she said confidently.

He nodded and jutted out his bottom lip. "Hmm. That would not be a problem with me, Meredith. I told you a lie about me having a wife. If things don't work out between you and Axel, I will take you."

"Nice to know I have options, Buluc. But I'm not sure I'm worthy of a god."

"No one is. But I will make an exception." He turned and walked back to sit at the fire.

"Are you for real?" she mumbled as she entered the kitchen.

To his credit, Buluc carried his bowl to the kitchen after he finished eating and even washed it. When she carried hers inside, he took it and cleaned it as well. Once, she noticed he squinted his eyes as he cocked his head in a kind of curiosity. The lines at the corners of those dark eyes appeared as if he might be suppressing a smile. She decided he was toying with her common sense and most likely was not as chauvinistic as he came across.

The firelight flickered in the breeze that rustled the palms nearby as Meredith joined Buluc on the deck. Once more, the darkness captured his attention as he dropped his arms to his sides. His face became void of expression. Before she sat down, his voice turned low and ominous.

"I want you to go inside. Axel has a gun in his nightstand. Wherever you put my weapons, I want you to put them under Axel's bed with the gun."

In spite of the evening humidity, she felt a chill. She came to stand beside him and studied his profile when he cut a sharp glare toward her then back to the darkness. "Now, Meredith. Do not come back out here. I will join you in a minute. Turn out the lanterns inside. Wait for me inside Axel's room away from the windows."

His voice, although calm, held a coarseness that spoke danger. She took two steps back, pivoted, and slowly walked inside to do the tasks he instructed her to do. Whatever had spooked him didn't involve his men, animals, or the weather. The threat turned the man into someone she was glad stayed behind to protect her. Axel trusted him, so she would, too.

Trust. What an odd thing to cross her mind at a time like this. Part of her was thrilled she could embrace the concept from two unlikely men that shouted danger. Why did they make her feel the safest she'd been in a long time? Even now, facing a possible threat, she felt like a hole had healed inside her and a kind of joy filled her, knowing this could happen.

She decided it was too quiet and Buluc might need help. Stepping out into the small hall between the bedrooms, Meredith wondered what was taking the Mayan so long to come inside. She decided to take a peek outside her protected area. Although the darkness was thick, the light from the firepit outside illuminated the inside of the combined living and kitchen area enough for her to notice Buluc was nowhere to be found, not inside or outside on the deck. A chill raced up her spine at the realization she was alone.

She moved out into the living room one slow step at a time. Whatever had spooked Buluc now attacked her ability to think straight. Wild scenarios flooded her imagination, ranging from a wild animal attack on

Buluc and dragging him into the jungle, to uninvited guests which included her ex-husband and two dangerous Russians.

The thought that Buluc may have become a tasty snack for a jaguar didn't make sense considering he would have been screaming for help, in spite of being a professed god. That left uninvited guests sneaking around. Lock the door popped into her head at the same time a shadow moved across the far end of the deck then another a few seconds later.

Where was Buluc? Had he stepped off into the darkness and someone silenced him, maybe permanently? Shouldn't Axel be back by now? Maybe it was him? That wouldn't explain the second shadow. Or the third one that just creeped along the edge of the deck. How many were out there?

The gun. In spite of never having used one, she realized having it might scare someone off or at least slow them down. She eased backward, never taking her eyes off things she couldn't see outside but believed were there. Pivoting to turn around, she slammed into a man whose arms went around her and pulled her tight to his chest. When she opened her mouth to scream, he quickly placed a hand over her lips to silence her.

"Hello, Meredith." It was Nathan, who smelled of sweat and grime. "You have been stirring up a great deal of trouble for me. Now I'm going to remove my hand, and I want you to be a good girl. Okay?"

She nodded. With her heart pounding in her ears, she stared in the eyes of a man she once thought she loved. A new kind of fear rose up inside her. His hand gently released then traced the outline of her jaw as he tilted his head. Even though his eyes softened, his arm grip did not.

"I would think being out here in the jungle you would have locks on the doors. Whoever that character was I saw on the deck a bit ago is gone. Who was he? Hired help? Certainly not a bodyguard since he took off into the jungle. Guess it's just us, sweetheart."

He released her, and she stepped back, taking a quick survey of who else might be inside.

"Nothing to say? Aren't you surprised to see me?" Nathan smirked like he did when he wanted to exert his strength over her by taking a step toward her at the same time she took two back. "I'm a little disappointed you didn't let me know about the winning lottery ticket before I signed the divorce decree. Your lawyer had a change of heart." He glanced over his shoulder at something she couldn't see. "Well, kind of, after my friends paid his family a visit. Anyway"—he waved his hand in impatience—"he told my friends where you might have gone. It wasn't hard to pick up your trail."

Yuri, one of the Russians stepped out of the darkest part of the room to reveal himself. "Sorry, Meredith. It wasn't supposed to happen this way. But your husband—"

"He's not my husband," she snapped.

"Of course. Once the police came to talk to us about your possible disappearance and murder, he negotiated another deal."

"You promised if I paid his debt, you'd protect me."

"I know. Sorry. We didn't know about the lottery ticket then or that he would need us to also help him. Now he owes us again, and one of you has to pay, or he may end up decomposing in a shallow grave in the jungle. You wouldn't want that, I'm sure."

"I'm thinking there would be worse things," she said flatly, causing Nathan to frown.

The Russian jutted out his thick lips as he approached her then twisted his mouth into a frustrated line. "I thought you might say that. Can't say I blame you. You're a nice lady. But Nathan needs you to give him half of the lottery money or…" He waved a gun toward the deck where the fire offered plenty of light. "Or we may have to bargain with other means."

The second Russian stepped up on the deck dragging someone else then gave her a shove. Sister Elena stumbled forward and caught herself on the back of one of the chairs. Her eyes lifted as to search inside the house as Meredith ran outside to gather the woman into her arms.

"Tell me what you want me to do," she sobbed as she stroked the back of the sister's head.

"Get inside," the second Russian ordered as he surveyed the jungle over his shoulder. "This place gives me the creeps." When the women didn't move fast enough, he jabbed Meredith in the side with his gun. "Now," he growled.

Sister Elena leaned into Meredith as she led her back inside just as the sky opened and started to rain. Once inside, Meredith led the sister to a chair. "Sister, are you hurt?"

"I don't know. Mostly tired, I think."

Meredith glanced at the clock and realized it was after eleven. "She is exhausted. I need to clean her up and put her to bed. Is that okay with you?" she asked the first Russian called Yuri.

"First, tell me where the man is who owns this place. I understand he brought you here."

"He went to town for supplies this morning by boat." Their asking meant they didn't have a clue what Axel was capable of. "The ocean is still a bit choppy from the hurricane. Probably won't make it back until tomorrow." She had no idea if that was true or not, but having them let down their guard sounded like a good idea. "He was going to try and find a truck to come back." Another lie.

Nathan snickered with a snort. "That won't help him. The road is a mess. Took forever. Doubt he'll have any luck getting a vehicle. Sonya Lavenworth secured us one, or we wouldn't have made it here."

"Figures you'd take up with the likes of someone like that," Meredith mumbled.

"Ha. Jealous? She and I hit it off pretty good. She said you came here and broke up her engagement with that Axel character she helped in Hollywood."

She decided to let him think she was jealous to help stroke his ego. He always did like to think of himself as a ladies' man. "I need to take care of Sister Elena. Can we talk in the morning? I'll stay with her. Crash on the couch, if you like. There's some soup if you want to warm it up. Close the screens, or you might end up with a slithery bed partner."

Nathan immediately did as she suggested. He was never one to enjoy nature. "This place makes my skin crawl. No way anyone would try and come over those roads tonight. They'd either end up being sacrificed to some Mayan god or driving off a cliff." He shivered.

The Mayan god comment gave her pleasure, thinking about Buluc. Since they hadn't mentioned seeing him after he disappeared in the jungle, she guessed he was nearby. Even though she hadn't known him or Axel very long, one thing she knew for sure was that they wouldn't leave her stranded and in danger for very long.

"What are you grinning about?" Nathan moaned as

he fastened a screen.

"Just hoping you didn't make any taboo moves to anger the Mayan gods." She helped Sister Elena stand and ushered her toward the bedroom. The sister gave a knowing look to her.

"Ha. Ha. Ha. Very funny. You always were superstitious."

"What are all those noises?" Yuri complained.

"Just the jungle. It's raining. Nothing will be moving about much," Sister Elena offered. She took Meredith's hand and tugged. "I want to rest awhile. Hmm. Is that howler monkey soup I smell?"

She hugged the woman. "Why, yes, it is. Would you like some?"

"Yes, please."

"Monkey soup. Are you kidding me?" moaned Nathan. "Think I'll pass."

"Go on." Yuri waved them off. "We can all use some sleep." His nose wrinkled as he sniffed the soup then walked away.

"Need some company, Meredith?" Nathan asked suggestively as his eyes raked over her.

She bristled and turned her back on him as she opened Axel's door for Sister Elena. She walked into the darkness. As she stepped through the door, she noticed a flashlight had been turned on at the nightstand. When she closed the door, someone grabbed her and shoved her against the door. A rough hand went over her mouth to prevent her from screaming.

"Shhhh," Buluc whispered then slowly removed his hand. He stepped back in time to see Sister Elena grab the flashlight and hurl it at his head. He dodged it in time, but it hit Meredith instead.

"Everything all right in there?" came Nathan's voice.

Sister Elena found Buluc's hand on her mouth as Meredith took care of the problem. "Yes. Fine. Dropped the flashlight is all. Couldn't find the lantern. Good now," she said, rubbing her cheek where the flashlight made contact. She hurried to the sister's side. "This is Buluc," she said as he released her.

The spunky lady gave the man a shove, but he barely budged. "I know who he is. And put some clothes on, Buluc, for goodness' sake." She put her hands on her hips and clicked her tongue.

"Then why did you try and hit me?"

"I didn't know who was in here."

"You know this man?" Meredith whispered in surprise.

"Yes, of course. He likes to scare the tourists with his 'I am Buluc Chabtan, the Mayan god of war, violence, and sudden death.' Blah. Blah. Blah."

"I have never harmed anyone."

"No, but you have caused many to hurt themselves getting away. Sacrilege!" she sniffed then sat down on the bed.

"Where did you go, Buluc?" Meredith asked, coming to stand next to him. They were all speaking in whispers. "I was worried."

"Did they hurt you?" he asked, going to the door where he pressed his ear.

"No. I'm more worried about her," she said, retrieving a washcloth from the adjoining half bath and sitting down beside her to clean her face and hands. "Do you hurt anywhere?" she asked, checking her arms where she saw some scratches.

"I fell and bumped my knee on a rock. That is going to give me trouble."

"I'll take a look."

The remarkable thing to Meredith was that the woman didn't act afraid, only mildly inconvenienced. She caught her up on the children and how they'd fared during the storm. The twins were asking for her. Axel's friend from the States had called to inquire about their safety and may have already arrived. She helped the woman lie back on the bed and lifted her legs to stretch out.

"I'll do what I need to, Sister Elena. Don't be afraid." Meredith pushed some strands of hair from the wrinkled face.

She reached for Meredith as she kneeled beside her. "I know you will. God is making a miracle. It just takes time. Axel will be here soon. I know it in my bones. And that half-dressed Mayan over there will watch over us until he arrives." Her eyelids drooped, and, in seconds, she was breathing peacefully.

Meredith went to stand by Buluc and put her ear to the door, too. "Are they sleeping?"

He stood up straight. "Not yet. One called Nathan has taken the room next to us. Is that your husband?"

"Not anymore. What about the others?" She faced him as he bent down to pick up the flashlight that had rolled under a chair after the attack. "Guess it's a good thing her aim was off?"

"She didn't mean to hit me. Must have been for you," he said matter-of-factly. "She is known for her quick temper."

Meredith sighed at his explanation. "Where did you

go earlier? You just disappeared."

"I could hear them coming. Their footsteps were loud, and the jungle creatures changed their voices to alert me. I slipped into the jungle and doubled back to climb through Axel's window. If you had stayed where I told you, then this would already be over." His tone did not indicate anger, only hinted at another possible outcome. "Do you wish for me to torture these men or kill them? I am very good at both. No one needs to know anything happened here. I also enjoy scaring people so they may run into the jungle and let the animals have a little fun." Even the darkness couldn't hide his smirk.

"Why don't we wait for Axel?"

"No. I promised to protect you, and he would never trust me again if I failed."

"He didn't say to kill them."

"He didn't say not to," he reminded her. He cracked the door and peered out. "This won't take long and then you can make tea, if you don't feel tired."

"But I—let me help you."

The cunning smile he leveled caused his midnight eyes to crease in amusement. "Stay out of my way—woman."

~ ~ ~ ~

Axel moved through the jungle quickly even though darkness fell. He made good time, thanks to his night vision goggles. When he spotted unexpected visitors stranded on the road, curiosity got the best of him. Two people arguing in the distance drew him to leave the safety of the jungle to venture back to the road. There, he found two people with a car mired up to the top of the wheels in mud. One was a woman who appeared familiar in spite of being dressed in black tactical gear. She yanked her hat off to reveal long blonde hair. The man turned his pen light around that reflected on his face. He recognized Mr. and Mrs. Pretend, or the Flynns, from the hotel. They'd left town, but, apparently, they were back. Although there was no way they would have gotten a flight out during the hurricane, it was interesting they were up here. Were they also hunting for Meredith?

He didn't have time to help them, and they would just slow him down. Given how they were dressed, he figured they knew how to take care of themselves. Right now, he needed to make sure Meredith was safe and find Sister Elena. If those two had any sense, they would get in their car and stay put until daylight. A jaguar let out a blood-curdling roar, making them scramble into the car. The big black cat strolled out of the jungle and jumped on the hood of their car and lay down. Maybe it was one of Sister Elena's miracles, the thought making him feel amused in spite of himself.

Another two hours put him near the compound where he discovered the intruders invaded his home. Where was Buluc? When the lights went on, he was able to see several of the men.

Axel circled around to try and figure out where all the players might be located before he acted. There was no sign of Buluc, but he figured he was nearby, maybe hiding somewhere for a surprise attack. Those were the kinds of antics that scared the tourists out of coming back to his nature reserve. There were warnings to avoid contact with native peoples there because they were protected just like the reserve.

A few lights came on, thanks to his solar power source. He could easily take that down and, unless they figured out how to use his solar lanterns, they'd be staggering in the dark. Then he saw Meredith standing toe to toe with the ex-husband. When he touched her face and arms, a rage welled up inside him, knowing how those same hands, fists, had hurt her when she didn't comply with his demands. She stepped back in retreat, but even from here, it was obvious, Nathan was having none of it.

Whatever the conversation was about, one of the Russians weighed in as he approached Meredith. He didn't appear to be as threatening as Nathan and Meredith appeared to be calm talking to him. He must be the one who helped her escape her ex in the first place. Even from here, there was no denying she stood her ground until another of the Russians went outside.

In seconds, he pulled Sister Elena up on the deck. She'd been on the opposite side of the deck where he couldn't see her. Meredith ran outside to her, gathering the woman in her arms. A sigh of relief at seeing them turned to vengeance a second later as the Russian dared jab his gun into her side. The man moved like someone uneasy, as he should be but probably wasn't because he expected a rescue for the women soon.

Working his way closer, Axel was able to hear part of the conversation until Nathan started slamming down screens for the night, causing him to miss what she said next. Meredith removed herself from the chaos to attend to Sister Elena by moving her to his bedroom. "Good girl," he whispered.

Since he knew the two women were safe, he decided to observe the three men. The only light outside was from the firepit that smoldered into tentacles of steam and would soon be extinguished. He guessed no one attended to that chore on purpose. Between the rain and thunder masking approaching sounds of two-legged threats, he felt like now he could move freely without being discovered.

He noticed Nathan had moved to the bedroom where the women disappeared and prepared himself to circle around to take him out if need be. The man put his lips close to the door, along with his hands, and asked if everything was all right. Axel couldn't resist a smile, realizing something frightened the women, and it most likely was Buluc. When Nathan went into the room next to them, he wondered how long it would be before Buluc lost patience and started cutting off fingers and toes to offer blood to the Mayan gods. There was a lot of speculation on whether Buluc had ever actually amputated anything important on a stranger, but Axel tended to believe that was a real possibility.

He'd told him many times that was illegal and he needed to chill out about the old ways. Buluc would shrug and agree to be more civilized in a modern world if he would keep tourists out of the jungle. There was a great deal of negotiating, especially if Axel had been sent to rescue nosey tourists. Mostly it was a theatrical show that worked to keep others from venturing into places held sacred by what was left of the traditional Mayans. He wasn't so sure how traditional Buluc really was or if it was just something he did for amusement.

At this moment, he was kind of hoping Nathan would end up losing something other than fingers and toes.

The two Russians were in discussion over something. When one went to lie on the couch and the other stood at the door before finding a more comfortable lookout point, he figured they'd be taking turns throughout the night. Those two weren't amateurs when it came to weapons or protection. He guessed they were former Spetsnaz, comparable to the Army Rangers in the US. They were as mean and tough as they came when in top military shape. These guys were a little older and heavier but still in good shape.

He guessed the Russian Mafia paid a good price for their service. Chances were they'd never trained for hand-to-hand combat in a rainforest. The Siberian tundra was a far cry from here.

Circling around to the back of the house, he found the window to his room and waited. With his night vision goggles, it was easy to see what was going on in the bedroom. Sister Elena lay on the bed. Buluc and Meredith were at the door. He couldn't hear what they were saying. Buluc reminded him of a patient father standing amused at a favored child as Meredith confronted him on an issue. The man wasn't used to a woman speaking her mind or standing up to him.

Axel made the sound of the local tree frog several times before Buluc jerked his head toward the window. He took a fighting stance and pushed Meredith behind him before moving on catlike feet toward the sound.

"What is it?"

"Shhh," Buluc said, holding up his finger to his lips. "We have company."

Meredith hurried to Sister Elena's bedside and waited.

"Buluc, unlock the screen, dammit."

Meredith covered her mouth in shock at the sound of his voice. Buluc fumbled with the latches, on purpose, Axel thought, then climbed inside. He raised his goggles and let his attention go to Meredith who ran into his arms. Lifting her off her feet, he kissed her, and she hugged his neck.

"I'm so glad to see you," she said as he lowered her feet to the floor.

Axel realized she had turned a corner in their relationship, and he was going to do everything in his power to make sure he didn't screw things up. "Are you okay? I watched from outside when your ex seemed to be trying to intimidate you."

"I promised to do whatever he wanted to save Sister Elena. I guess her miracle might not happen after all. They would have hurt her."

Buluc sniffed. "You forget I was here to protect you both."

Both Meredith and Axel shared an amused glance, much to the Mayan's disgust.

"Thank you, my friend. I knew you were close. No way you would have left two fine women to fend for themselves," Axel asserted.

"Right," he said as he raised a stubborn chin. "Now we should kill this man next door and take him to the jungle."

"I guess the fire ants would take care of most of him," Axel said off-handedly.

"I would like to watch," Buluc said with enthusiasm.

Meredith sucked in her breath. "I can't believe what I'm hearing. You can't kill him."

"She is what you call"—Buluc tapped his chin as if trying to remember—"buzz-kill."

Axel pulled her into his side and kissed her temple. "He's just teasing," he admitted.

Meredith shifted her eyes to the solemn Buluc as if waiting for him to admit the same thing. Instead, he said, "I was not teasing."

Axel poked him in the side that wasn't wounded.

"I mean, I will not feed him to the ants."

She continued to stare menacingly at him.

"Sorry. That's all I got for you, Meredith. You must remember I am used to having a human sacrifice."

Axel couldn't help but be amused at her expression. Buluc was just messing with her, but the Mayan was a dangerous man when cornered or crossed.

Walking over to the bed, he squatted and laid his hand on Sister Elena's that rested on her chest. Her eyes fluttered open, and her shining eyes warmed his heart.

"You have come for me."

"I have. Got any miracles we can use? You know— just in case."

"I am still waiting for a miracle. Things that are worthwhile are not easy. Stop whining and go kick some butt." She grinned.

"Sister! Language!" he said, pinching her cheek. Standing, he bent down and kissed her forehead. "Get some rest. Everything will be fine." Taking his hand, she kissed the back and then held it to her cheek. Soon her eyes closed and she was sleeping again.

Meredith put her arm around him, drawing his attention to her. "I checked her over. She is not hurt.

Her knees will probably be sore for a while, since she fell. But her heart and blood pressure were strong. I want to check her knees out when we get back. Will that be okay with you?"

"Yes. Thank you, Meredith." He moved back to stand with Buluc. "What ya say we pay the easy one a visit."

"What can I do?" she said anxiously.

Buluc was already slipping out the window when Axel shared the plan.

~ ~ ~ ~

Resting her forehead against the door and her hand on the doorknob, Meredith once again questioned her mental state when she decided to hide a billion-dollar lottery ticket and escape with the help of a couple of Russian thugs. But the upside was the people she crossed paths with. The experience just may lead to a happy life in the end. She glanced back at the sister, who slept soundly, before taking a deep breath and opening the door.

Stepping out into the hall, the Russian on guard glanced at her and moved her way. She pushed her hair behind her ears and tried to appear seductive. "Just wanted to talk to Nathan. Maybe he would like to renegotiate a few things."

The Russian glanced toward Nathan's room and nodded his okay.

Once he returned to guard duty, Meredith tapped lightly on the door. Her stomach turned, thinking about what she was about to do. The thought of him touching her caused her to shiver in spite of the warm humidity.

The light shone under the door. His footsteps drew near. Cracking the door to peer out, he arched an eyebrow, followed by a smirk then opened it wider. A dim lightbulb caused shadows to form on his face, revealing he needed a shave.

"I knew you missed me." He reached out and pulled her into his arms.

When he tried to kiss her, she turned her head.

"Playing hard to get?" Running his hand through her hair then down her cheek, he kissed her mouth in spite of the protest. "Doesn't matter. I'm used to you doing that. Always ended up satisfying for both of us."

"Slow down. We've got all night," she said, forcing herself to soften her voice as she looked into his eyes. "I'm feeling unsure about all this. You can't come here, threaten me into submission, and expect me to feel— attracted to you." She forced a sensual smile, reached back to close the door, and locked it.

"I like where this is headed. Why don't you get out of those clothes?"

Meredith ran her hands down his chest all the way to the waist of his pants. "You first. I"— she nibbled his ear—"want to see you, touch you."

She had never seen anyone drop their pants and slip out of their shirt so fast in their life.

"Now, let me help you," he said, reaching for the top button of her shirt.

Pushing his hands away, she stepped back and opened the first button. "Watch me, Nathan." She wet her lips, knowing she now had his undivided attention. "You remember all those times you hit me?"

He tilted his head and squinted his eyes.

"I think maybe a little payback is in order."

A frown crossed his face.

"Then I guess you never learned your lesson. I want you tonight, and I'm sure you feel the same."

"I'm thinking you got your signals crossed, Nathan," Axel whispered in his ear.

Nathan spun around and ran into the naked, painted chest of Buluc. His terrified surprise made Meredith laugh. Knowing she'd kept him busy long enough for her friends to sneak in without detection gave her great satisfaction. They had him gagged and tied within seconds before pushing him down on the bed. With so much face paint on, no one would ever recognize Buluc. Axel was definitely camouflaged enough to keep his identity a secret if need be.

She walked to the bed and eyed her ex-husband then crossed her arms across her chest.

"About the money. You're not getting any of it. I made a trust for that money, and Sister Elena gets a pretty big chunk of it. At least she won't waste it like you would gambling. You think those guys out there are going to leave you alone? They were ready to let the authorities think you killed me. Their bosses are going to think of this as an embarrassment."

"That's right, Nathan. You'd better find you another set of friends. With any luck, the authorities will be here by tomorrow to cart your ass off."

Buluc took his long knife and held it to Nathan's head before sawing off a chunk of his hair. This made the man try to cry out beneath the gag. It led to the Mayan lowering the knife to his throat. "You are very noisy," he growled.

Nathan's eyes bulged as he turned them to Meredith. For once, he was pleading for help. Part of her wanted to participate; the other part just wanted to enjoy the look of horror on his face.

Finally, she spoke. "I want you to promise not to make a sound, Nathan." He nodded vigorously. "Because, if you do, my friend here wants to drop you in the jungle on a fire anthill. It would be most unpleasant. Can I trust you to be quiet? If any harm comes to us, you'll never make it out of here alive. Do you understand?"

Once more, he nodded vigorously. She was sure there were tears in his eyes this time.

"And if any harm comes to Sister Elena, I promise there will be hell to pay," she declared. "Gentlemen, do you have anything you'd like to add?"

Buluc went to the window where he'd left a small tube of something. He squirted it up and down Nathan's legs. "Honey," he said drily.

Axel took out a transparent cup the size of a medicine container. Something moved under the lid. "Fire ants." He sat the container down between his legs. "I wouldn't knock that over if I were you."

A moan escaped through the gag as Nathan appeared panicked with increased sweating. Meredith reached down and patted his leg. "I'm sure everything will be fine. We'll be back to release you later." She accidently turned the container over, causing him nearly to jump out of his skin. Righting the flip, she offered him a sad expression. "Oops. Sorry about that. Lid is still on tight, babe. Now, be a good boy."

Together, the three moved to the open window.

CHAPTER 31

One of the Russians tapped on Meredith's door. She cracked it open after she'd ruffled her hair into a mess and unfastened several buttons. With a weak smile and an attempt to rebutton her blouse, she gripped the door as if struggling to stand.

"I heard a commotion. I thought you were with the ex." His voice always sounded like he needed to clear his throat. His eyes took her in from head to toe. "Are you okay?"

"I-I think so. He's not an easy man to talk to, Yuri." She had dabbed a spot of spit at the corner of her eye for a special effect. The man had been fairly kind to her when she'd asked for help.

He peered around her, into the room. "The old lady okay?"

"Not really. She's exhausted and her knees are badly bruised. I think she needs a doctor."

Looking toward Nathan's door, he took a step backward in that direction.

"Yuri, do you think I could make myself a cup of

tea?"

He stopped and wasn't shy about exploring her body with his narrowed gaze.

"Join me," she urged. "Maybe we could talk about a safe way to get out of here."

"Good. Yes. Make the tea." He motioned for her to walk out ahead of him.

Gently, she closed the door and walked into the living room toward the kitchen. He followed a little too close, so, when she stopped suddenly, he ran into her, placing his arms around her. Spinning her around, he gave a lopsided grin that revealed a missing tooth. Then he froze as Axel pushed a gun to the back of his neck.

"I'm not sure you are much of a Boy Scout, so what ya say you take your hands off the lady and extend your arms out like an airplane."

The Russian yelled loud enough to wake the dead as he jumped to the side and spun around with his gun in hand. Grabbing his neck with his free hand, he pulled out a pin-like spine. His eyes widened when he saw Buluc standing near the other Russian who was gagged and bound on the couch.

Axel gave a devious grin. "Nighty night, loser." The Russian collapsed onto the floor, shaking the room hard enough to rattle a few pictures on the wall. "Meredith?"

"I'm good."

He holstered his weapon and stepped closer then she fell into his arms and laid her head on his shoulder. "I'm so glad you're here."

"I could have taken care of them," Buluc insisted as he laid his blowgun on the table. He poked the second Russian who was wide awake and looking terrified at the painted Mayan looming over him. "My way was more entertaining."

Meredith couldn't help herself and burst out laughing which caused Buluc to screw up his lips to the side in a kind of amusement.

~ ~ ~ ~

Even though Buluc didn't want to admit it, his activity had taken a toll on him. With only a little coaxing, he decided a sling would be okay for a while, but only until his men returned. Then he must demonstrate his powers to heal and return to normal. But, by morning, he was sleeping like a baby in the hammock outside. He refused to come inside the night before after the rain stopped. He was protected in a screened-in porch so there was no concern about wild animals.

Axel had built up the fire in case they had company. He'd shared about the fake married couple being stuck on the road then cornered by the black cat. The lack of sleep was weighing on him, and Meredith kept nodding off on the rattan love seat in the living room. Both Russians were secured and no longer a threat to them.

Nathan had made enough noise for them to remove what he thought were fire ants so he finally settled down. In truth, they were just some tiny bugs he'd scooped up with dirt outside the window. He, too, fell asleep, leaving him the only one to keep track of everyone, including the two stranded at their car.

When daybreak broke, he asked Buluc to take over for him in order to take a nap. An hour later, he was refreshed and found Meredith in the kitchen fixing skillet toast and coffee.

"It was all I found." She passed him a plate, and they

followed Buluc outside to eat.

The Russians sat on the edge of the deck with Nathan, handcuffed and their feet tied, but were able to eat some of the toast. They often argued among themselves, and Axel figured they were plotting how they were going to overtake and outwit their current situation. Sister Elena joined them and, with the help of a cane he found, she got along good as new.

As often happens after a hard rain, the day following was sunny and beautiful. The rainforest had once more come alive, and the sound of distant waves crashing onto the beach helped center himself. Looking at Meredith stretched out in a chaise lounge, sipping coffee, gave him the feeling that life was nearly complete. Would she stay on now if this loose end could be tied up?

Buluc squinted at something in the jungle and raised his chin for Axel to be alert. Both men retrieved their weapons and asked Meredith to help Sister Elena move closer to the door.

"What is it? I don't see anything."

"How many?" Axel asked Buluc.

"More than four. Maybe three more. Could be my men."

"All of them?"

"No." Buluc cocked his head at the prisoners. "Maybe those crocodiles that got moved around from their home during the hurricane. Happens every time. Hungry." He nodded toward the terrified guests tied and helpless. "Crocs like white meat."

A sharp whistle three times echoed across the camp. Their three captives struggled to stand since they were tethered to the railing posts. Staring into the tree line started a litany of "just release us, we'll help, what is it?"

"Shut up," Axel growled. He then whistled back.

"Good lord," Nathan gasped. "There's a whole bunch of them," he said, twisting around. "Meredith, help me. I promise I'll never bother you again. Ever. You can keep all the money."

The Russians quickly agreed to do the same.

"Deal. Let me handle this. Buluc, maybe you can translate."

Axel knew the Mayans coming into the clearing. They were Buluc's men and his friends as well. They were also painted for a fight, jabbing and talking smack to three people. Two of them were the fake married couple. The third had a familiar stride and didn't appear to be in distress. As a matter of fact, he appeared to be with Buluc's men.

"Jake? Is that you?"

Carrying an M4 Carbine like he was going into combat, his friend from the old days walked with four of the Mayans he'd come to know over the last few years. The other two were the couple he left stranded on the road with a jungle cat making himself at home on the hood of their Land Rover. He was clothed much like himself to blend into his surroundings. The unlikely married couple walked unconcerned as they accompanied his friends. Upon closer inspection and to his surprise, they also carried some serious firepower. They stepped upon the deck, the Mayans staying spread out around the compound as if they might be waiting for someone else.

"Hey, buddy," Jake said, extending his free hand. "Bet you're surprised to see me."

"That's putting it mildly." Axel grabbed his hand and remembered the vise grip of his friend.

Sister Elena clapped her hands in excitement and motioned for Jake to come to her. He rushed to her side and kneeled down so she could hug him. "My other son has come home." Her voice was joyful as she patted his cheeks. "Thank you for coming."

He stood. "I see you guys have everything under control." He nodded toward the familiar couple who had been a thorn in his side. "Well, except maybe these two." Jake pointed toward the Flynns.

The man stepped forward. "I'm Special Agent Jonas, and this is my partner, Special Agent Taylor." He fished out his ID as he took a moment to do a visual inspection of the prisoners. "We've been tracking the Russians for about six months. Racketeering, money laundering, fraud, and criminal conspiracy are just a few of my favorite things," he said, frowning at the Russians who started speaking in their native tongue to him.

Agent Taylor snapped back in Russian and, whatever she said, they decided not to speak further. When she turned back to the others, she took on a serious, non-emotional expression.

"I found out after the last time I talked to you these two feds were really after Nathan, since he skipped town. We figured since Meredith hit the big time, he'd be coming after her. It wasn't hard picking up her trail."

"Hey!" Nathan shouted. "Get me out of here and take me home. I'll testify against these guys. I've got lots to tell you."

Agent Jonas exhaled. "As I said, 'idiot.' He knew what he was doing, but we need his testimony. When he skipped town after the Russians posted his bail, we had no choice but to hunt Meredith down." He shifted his attention to her. "We wanted to make sure you were okay because there was a chance he might kidnap you and well, I guess you can figure out the rest."

"How did you find me?" she asked, coming to stand next to Sister Elena.

"By accident. We thought maybe you were involved. Reached out to one of your girlfriends from Arcadia Valley where you used to live. They thought you were in danger and cooperated with us. Once we had filled in the missing pieces, it wasn't difficult."

"Sorry, Meredith. I got it all wrong," Jake confessed then turned to Axel. "I came out here as quick as I could. By then, I knew who Taylor and Jonas were and what they were trying to do. You had already taken Meredith to hide. That Sonya chick had a lot of tips sent in saying they'd seen you. She told Nathan and the Russians where you were mostly headed."

"Will Sonya face charges?" It was Axel.

Jonas shook his head. "Not likely. She would draw too much attention and shut down any other operations we have underway. Someone is with her even as we speak about keeping her mouth shut or we will press charges. That wouldn't look good for America's sweetheart or for her career."

"And Meredith? Is she in trouble?" Axel asked.

Agent Taylor stepped forward. "After we friended you and followed you, we ascertained you had nothing to do with their operations. You were in danger from your ex-husband and in possession of a lot of money, none of which he had any rights to. However, you may face charges concerning having the Russians assist you in leaving."

Meredith opened her mouth to speak but was cut off.

"It is a matter we can work with considering the abuse and other crimes your ex is involved in." Agent Taylor's expression softened.

"An innocent victim," Axel chimed in.

"Exactly."

Buluc joined the group and rushed toward Jake who quickly grabbed the Mayan and gave him a hug that caused him to wince with pain. "Oh, sorry. Still scaring the dickens out of college eco-terrorists?"

"You know each other?" Meredith asked in amazement.

Jake slipped his arm around the Mayan's shoulder. "Hell, yeah. We went to Princeton together."

"Princeton University? As in Ivy League?" She discovered Buluc with new eyes. "What was your major?"

"Biodiversity," Buluc quipped. "I didn't finish."

"Actually, he was kicked out." Jake laughed.

"It was too cold," he explained.

"Of course, it was. You went around dressed like you are now. You used a blow gun to hunt on campus."

"I didn't want to get out of practice."

When all the players had been explained, Agent Jonas was able to call in support to remove the prisoners. Agent Jonas thanked Axel and Buluc for their help and promised to send the helicopter back to pick them up later in the day.

"I must go," Buluc said as his men started back toward the jungle. He waited until they were out of sight before letting Meredith give him the tetanus shot. "I have much to do. Meredith, thank you for helping me and for the medicine. Remember what I told you about living with me once you are married."

She stepped closer and hugged him gently. "I will remember. Thank you for protecting me while Axel was gone."

Raising his chin in a show of pride, he extended his hand toward Axel. They grasped each other's forearm. "Until next time, brother."

"Next time," Axel said quietly. Both men turned to look at Meredith who helped Sister Elena to her feet and led her to the men.

"Don't let her leave," Buluc said flatly then walked away toward the jungle.

Axel continue to study the two women who hooked their arms together. "I won't," he said under his breath. "But it might take a miracle."

CHAPTER 32

Six months later

"Hurry, children," Sister Elena said, clapping her hands. "Everyone dressed?"

Rosa and Pedro scooted in front of her, waiting for inspection. "How do we look?"

Sister Elena dabbed at her eyes. "Beautiful," she said then added, "and handsome, Pedro." The other children scampered past her and ran toward the backyard that had been transformed into a Garden of Eden. Chairs were positioned in rows and filled with friends, new and old. Some wore suits or tropical clothing, and a few barely wore clothes at all.

Axel, dressed in a suit and tie, stood nervously next to his best friend Jake Thorn at the front, along with the local judge. Guests filed in to sit in the first few rows of seats. Next came Sister Elena holding the hands of Rosa and Pedro. The three of them stood at the front, opposite of Axel. The twins, for once, waited patiently as they wore big smiles.

Someone started the recording of "Canon in D," by Pachelbel. Everyone stood and watched Meredith Marshall, dressed in a slim, floor-length wedding dress descend the steps from the newly painted orphanage. Her escort was none other than Buluc Chabtan, the Mayan god of war. He held his head held high and wore his best face paint and clothes, what there was of them, as he looped Meredith's hand through his arm.

He leaned in and whispered, "You can do better. I am a much better choice."

"I do not deserve a god, Buluc," she reminded him.

"This is true." He stole an appreciative glance at her and smiled. "You are beautiful."

"Let's go."

Axel was not given to emotion, for the most part, but seeing Meredith walk down the aisle in front of his friends with the grace and beauty of a queen, he couldn't help but beam at the woman he loved more than life itself. It was a heady experience to feel like this.

"Who gives this woman in marriage?" the judge asked.

"Buluc Chabtan, the Mayan god of war. Who do you think?" he snapped impatiently.

"It's tradition to ask, Buluc," she said out of the corner of her mouth.

"Oh. Sister Elena and her protector."

The judge's eyebrows rose as his mouth turned down in a frown. He kept it short considering the children would call out their support from time to time.

"I now pronounce you man and wife. You may kiss the bride," he declared.

Axel slipped his arm around Meredith and pulled her close. Their lips connected long enough that someone yelled, "Get a room, Axel." Laughter broke out as they separated and laughed, too.

The judge held up his hands and announced one more thing. "Since these two have decided to become one, they have also started adoption proceedings for Rosa and Pedro. Children come stand in front of me."

They quickly hurried to hold the hands of Meredith and Axel, staring up at them.

"As of today, do you, Rosa, and you, Pedro, take these two to be your lawful parents as long as you both shall live?"

They jumped up and down until the judge intervened.

"You have to answer."

"Yes. Yes. Yes." They giggled in unison.

The audience burst into cheers and tears at the same time. Even Buluc was said to have dabbed his eyes at the surprise.

"I now pronounce you a family. May God bless you. You're going to need it."

The applause was long and loud as Meredith and Axel embraced their children.

"Can we call you Mommy and Daddy now?" Rosa asked.

Axel picked up the little girl and kissed her as Meredith bent over to tousle the little boy's hair. "You most certainly can."

Sister Elena pointed to the new sign on the entrance of the garden. "I told you we'd get a miracle. Thanks to Meredith, we are debt free, and the clinic is opening full-time next week."

Several of Buluc's men pulled the covering free to reveal the words: House of Miracles.

"I love you," Axel whispered in her ear.

"Any chance we can make a few more little miracles?"

"Sister Elena is counting on it," he said, leaning in for another kiss.

ABOUT TIERNEY JAMES
Adventure, Thriller & Romantic Suspense Author

Tierney James decided to become a full-time writer after working in education for over thirty years. Besides serving as a Solar System Ambassador for NASA's Jet Propulsion Lab, and attending Space Camp for Educators, Tierney served as a Geo-teacher for National Geographic. Her love of travel and cultures took her on adventures throughout Africa, Asia and Europe. From the Great Wall of China to floating the Okavango Delta of Botswana, Tierney weaves her unique experiences into the adventures she loves to write. Living on a Native American reservation and in a mining town, fuels the characters in the Enigma and Wind Dancer series. Now with over twenty books under her belt, Tierney feels there is no stopping her now.

After moving to Oklahoma, the love of teaching continued in her marketing and writing workshops along with the creation of educational materials and children's books. She likes to tell people a little lipstick and danger makes the world go round. http://www.tierneyjames.com Speaking at conferences, book clubs, school functions, church and community groups are a few of the things Tierney enjoys doing when not writing her next adventure. She also helps beginning writers in their quest to becoming a published author through her workshops and classes. Family, an adopted dog and gardening fill her life with plenty of laughter to share with others.

Tierney has been an Amazon #1 Best Selling author and won numerous awards for her work.

OTHER PUBLICATIONS BY TIERNEY JAMES

The Enigma Series Vol. 1-8
Martyrs Never Die
Invisible Goodbye
The Knight Before Chaos
Black Mamba
Kifaru
Rooftop Angels
The Winds of Deception
An Unlikely Hero

The Dark Side Series
Dark Side of Noon
Dark Side of Morning

Stand Alone Books
The Rescued Heart
Dance of the Devil's Trill
Turnback Creek
Lipstick & Danger – A Collection of Short Stories When Escape is Your Only Option

Other
How to Market a Book Someone Besides Your Mother Will Read
There's a Superhero in the Library
Zombie Meatloaf
Mission K-9 Rescue
African Safari: A Thematic Lesson Book for Teachers

From the Author

Thanks for following along in each adventure I write. I'd love for you to follow me on social media as well.

Facebook:
https://www.facebook.com/AuthorTierneyJames/

Facebook Reader Group:
https://www.facebook.com/groups/2430789897157949

Amazon:
https://www.amazon.com/Tierney-James/e/B00C1FB19Q

Twitter:
https://twitter.com/TierneyJames1

Website:
http://www.tierneyjames.com (Please sign up for my newsletter on the home page)

Pinterest:
https://www.pinterest.com/ptierneyjames/

Instagram:
www.tierneyjames7